# TANGLED RETRIBUTION

CREDITS

Once again I want to thank all my colleagues in East Hampshire
Writers who listened to me reading my work and made many helpful
ideas and suggestions.  Finally, I owe thanks again to John Owen
Smith who typeset the book and put it into a neat and tidy volume.


AUTHOR

Jim Morley has sailed and raced small boats all his life.  He spent
forty years in farming and forestry, combining this with a career in
freelance writing.
    He has published three novels, reflecting his interest in boats and
also rural matters.  He lives near Petersfield in Hampshire and sails a
small family cruising yacht on Chichester Harbour.


COVER: Sunset in the Anchorage by J. Morley.

# TANGLED RETRIBUTION

*James Morley*

**Tangled Retribution**
First published 2012

Published by Benhams Books, 1 Fir Cottage, Greatham, Liss, Hampshire GU33 6BB

Typeset by John Owen Smith




ISBN 978-0-9548880-6-0

Printed by CreateSpace

# PROLOGUE

The girl crouched in a corner of the room, her faced twisted in misery, her body convulsed. Outside the building a sub-tropical storm raged. The yacht club guests eyed the girl uneasily as they passed through the room. Why was this pretty little thing so distraught in this typical laid-back Australian celebration? This was party time in Melbourne. A happy few hours reserved for dancing, singing and above all drinking.

One young couple were not indifferent. They stopped in their tracks when they saw the other. Within the yacht club came the sound of jollity, stomping feet and heavy metal rock music. The rain pounded above on the thin roof of the annexe.

'Oh, sweetheart, what's happened?' the woman broke away from her companion and flung her arms around the girl.

She turned and stared at her comforter with a face distorted and reddened with tears. 'Oh, Nicky, that man murdered her,' she sobbed. 'He's the one that killed my baby.'

'But why?'

'He thinks the law can't touch him and…I can't help it…I still love him.'

The other woman spoke. 'You can't feel for him. Not if he really did that.'

'I do, I do,' the girl wailed.

The man spoke. His voice was English with a trace of another accent. 'Come on Nick, we'll find that bastard and sort him out.'

'Not before time,' replied Nicky.

# CHAPTER 1

'This is it – we've got here,' said Tom as he parked the Renault outside the entrance of the maternity unit. 'How are you?' he turned to look at Emily leaning back in the passenger seat nursing her baby bump.

'What do you think, you idiot – it's bloody agony.' Emily groaned.

Tom was not fazed by this. He had already been briefed that part of his function that night was to be a target for his wife's pain and irritation.

'Sit tight, I'll fetch help,' he called as he ran for the entrance.

'Can your wife walk?' asked the receptionist.

'I'm not sure – we've not done this before.'

'If you're doubtful, take one of those wheelchairs.' The receptionist jabbed her thumb towards the far wall and resumed reading her magazine.

Tom grabbed a wheelchair and trundled it back through the entrance.

'What the hell's that for?' Emily gasped. 'Oh God this is bloody horrible – ahhh.'

'I thought it would make it easier for you.' Tom by now was wholly outside his comfort zone and he was beginning to panic.

'Well you can bloody think different. Sitting down is even worse – I'll walk.'

Emily's waters had broken and the early contractions had started, but she was still able to walk as they were guided into the maternity suite. Emily stood unsteadily next to the birthing bed and the midwife introduced herself. She was a pretty Afro-Caribbean woman who looked far too young in Tom's eyes.

'Have you done a lot of this?' he asked anxiously.

'Should think so,' the midwife giggled. 'Fetched out thirty or so here and had two of my own.' She turned to Emily. 'All right, dear. How's it going and how many contractions?'

Emily groaned in pain. 'They keep coming. Can't you do something?'

Tom realised he would have to readjust his male chauvinist prejudices. He had visualised a midwife as an ageing virgin spinster compensating for her loss by helping other's children into the world.

Emily had relaxed temporarily and was staring blearily at the girl. 'Hey, I've seen you at Hamble – you sail.'

'I crew for my husband in his dinghy, but you are the gold medal winner?'

'She certainly is,' Tom grinned.

'Then we're going to take special care of you and the new arrival. Do you know if it's boy or girl?'

'The scan says boy,' Emily croaked.

Tom wanted to distract Emily from the present. He asked the midwife. 'Do you know what's happening in the double Trans Atlantic?'

'Yes,' she replied. 'Last we heard *Avocet* our local boat is winning with four hundred miles to go.'

'That's great,' said Emily in more like her normal voice. 'You see her skipper is a distant relation of my mum. We only found out a few months back.'

'He's Danish isn't he?'

'Yes, so's my…aahrr, God, aahooo,' Emily gasped then screamed. Her face twisted with her pain.

Tom was horrified. He loved his wife and now his actions had put her in this hell. He had been briefed at length. He had been given a two page birth plan but all this was frightening and alien. He began to panic but he knew he must be controlled and resist showing it.

'Right, time for the gas and air' said the midwife briskly. 'We're on our way. Start count down – ten minute gun.'

'Not as quick as that surely?' asked Tom. He felt utterly surreal and out of touch.

'We'll be lucky,' Emily gasped. 'Stop grinning, you prat. You are going to do your share and you can forget about sex for weeks or months probably.'

'I wasn't grinning!' he replied. Tom didn't really care about her threat. He was too worried.

The midwife helped Emily onto the bed and turned to wink. The intercom phone rang. 'Mr Stoneman I think you need to move your car. It's in the way of the ambulance.'


It was several hours later that a mentally shattered Tom ran down the hospital corridor for the payphone. The hospital had offered a portable one by the bedside. Tom by nature did not favour showing his emotions in front of hospital staff. Mobiles were not
encouraged and luckily he had his phone card. This place smelt of

floor polish and disinfectant and the background of moans and groans from the other birth rooms was spooky. The highly polished floor was almost his downfall; nearly slipping flat on his face before he reached the phone.

He called his parents and then Emily's parents and Emily's half-sister, Sarah.

'She's done it. He's a boy, seven and a half pounds, and he's going to be Peter.'

He staggered giddily back to the room. Emily sat up in bed with the tiny bundle in her arms his face resting on her naked breast. Tom bent down and kissed his wife's dark hair and then ran a finger lightly over the little face. Did he imagine it? No, he was certain that the little face seemed to smile back. Tom felt warmth, happiness and a sense of achievement and incredibly he found himself wiping away tears. He looked at Emily; her own face registered both exhaustion and supreme tranquillity.

She smiled at him. 'Have you told everyone?'

'Yes.'

'Everyone? Did you ring Chloe?'

'No.'

'I thought not. All right, do it now. She's got a right to know. Do it with this phone we've got here.' Emily lapsed into a dreamlike exhaustion.

Tom gritted his teeth and rang the number; anything to keep his wife happy.


'I want to see if that house is warm enough,' said Kirsten. 'It's bloody cold out there.'

Steve couldn't argue with that. It was mid-April and cold with an icy east wind blast.

'Are you sure poor Tom wants a mother-in-law bossing him around?'

'I've got duty to our daughter and Tom doesn't see me that way,' said Kirsten.

Steve grunted. As a man he remained unconvinced. At the same time it felt good. His youngest daughter had a child, a boy; his grandson. Emily deserved this joy. She had earned it: rising young barrister, Olympic gold medallist and long before that the victim of abduction by that lunatic cult. If anyone deserved a quiet and settled life it was his Emily. He went to the kitchen to dig out the celebratory Champagne bottle and tucked it in a bag for the twenty mile journey from South Marshall in Sussex to Emily and Tom's cottage in Bishops Sutton, the little village just outside Alresford in Hampshire. He could hear Kirsten warming up the car outside on the drive.

He crossed to his study and had one more look at the computer. He had been tracking the marathon double trans-Atlantic Race held between nine competing maxi-yachts. This was the first long distance offshore race of the season. With two hundred miles to go to the finish at Plymouth *Avocet Computers* had a substantial lead or she should have. He stared at the online chart. *Avocet* had barely moved in the last three hours and *Qualistores* was beginning to catch her. Steve had an interest in this, in fact a double interest. *Avocet's* skipper was Alfred Ollavasen a distant Danish cousin of Kirsten, while *Avocet's* sails had been designed and cut by Steve's own firm: Easterbroke of Chichester. There was no report from *Avocet* but it looked as if something had broken. Dismasting? Surely not, the rigging on these yachts was belt and braces stuff and anyway it wasn't blowing that hard out there. Avocet Computers the yacht's sponsors was a vast concern based in Switzerland. Qualistores was that greedy retail empire colonising every high street.

'Steve, come on we're off,' Kirsten shouted.


'Oh, he's sooo beautiful,' Kirsten gushed while looking down at the little form.

'Of course he is.' Emily lay full length on the sofa the baby in her arms. 'He looks like Tom with a bit of Dad as well.'

'Two handsome guys,' said Tom.

'Mum,' asked Emily. 'What was I like as a baby?'

Steve laughed. 'You didn't give us a minute's peace through twenty four hours and you had a mighty pair of lungs.'

It was a magic moment. The Champagne fizzed and the cottage was warm with an open log fire in the front room. 'Tony says I can take as much time off work as I like,' said Emily. 'Trouble is I will need cases; barristers are technically self-employed although Tony is going to pass me work from his list.'

Tony Travis QC was Emily's mentor and Steve knew that his daughter was already making a big impression on the law court scene. She had only little local cases to
prosecute or defend so far, but her preparation and courtroom skills were already making older barristers and judges for that matter, sit up and take notice.

The baby suddenly stirred and gave forth a wail. 'See what I mean,' said Kirsten. 'That's what you were like twenty four seven.'

'He's hungry,' Emily sat up. 'Come on little Pete. Time for more tit.' She picked up the baby and undid her shirt.

'Do you have to be so crude?' said Steve.

'Why are you still such a prude?' Kirsten glared at him. 'You should know by now that she's only winding you up and you fall for it every time.'

'She picks up a lot of that from Chloe,' said Tom. 'You know; Kiwi; tell it as it is.'

'I can't imagine Chloe suckling a baby.' Emily sniggered.

'Are you going to stick with the breast feeding?' Kirsten asked.

'For the moment, yes.'

Tom laughed. 'I'd love to see you stop yapping in court and fasten the little one onto a nipple in front of the judge and all.'

'You are living in a world of fantasy,' said Kirsten.

'No,' said Emily 'I reckon Peter will be off the breast and well into bottles and soft stuff before I go back to the law.'

'When do you get back to work, Tom?' asked Steve.

'The firm says I can take a fortnight by law without affecting my annual leave, but I'll have to go back soon; we're busy right now.'

'Josie, it doesn't make sense,' said David Manning. He was sitting in the yacht club watching the computer screen.

His girl friend put an arm around him. 'Have they sent a mayday signal?'

'No, nothing; they are making some sort of way, but it's only ten miles in the last six hours. So *Qualistores* is going to take the race and that bastard Crickerman is going to take the glory.'

'I thought you said a sports reporter had to be impartial.'

Dave leaned across and hugged Josie. 'I try to write impartial but I don't have to think it. Come on let's go and get a drink. I need one.'

They walked into the yacht club bar. The room was crowded with happy drinkers and echoing with their chatter. Dave spotted a fellow New Zealander. Chloe Te Koote was a personality that awed any room she stood in and a total maverick. A Maori serving as a major in the British army was one thing, but added to that an ill-concealed lesbian. Chloe was big in every sense: stocky in build, dressed in bulky denim, with dark hair and Anglo-Polynesian features. She was muscular, self-confident and domineering. None of this mattered to Dave. Chloe was the world's number one woman yacht helm with an Olympic gold won.

'Dave,' Chloe shrieked making half the customers jump. 'Dave, I've news. Emily's dropped her kiddy. He's a boy seven and half pounds.'

'Are they all OK?' asked Dave. 'After everything she went through in Olifa it would be awful if it went wrong now.'

'Naah, she and that husband of hers have put it all behind them.'

Dave smiled inwardly. The extrovert Chloe had never really clicked with Tom. But Chloe was Emily's gold medal skipper in the three girl match racing contest along with fellow crew member Erin. Dave wouldn't forget that dramatic last race in a hurry.

'What are you drinking, Chlo?'

'Thanks, another pint o' that real ale bitter please.'

Dave carried two pints of ale and Josie's red wine back to the table that Chloe had already grabbed. 'How's the Atlantic race going?' asked Chloe.

'Not so good,' said Dave. '*Avocet's* been disabled and that shit

Crickerman is going to take the race.'

'Not bad news to me, mate,' said Chloe. 'You know my partner, Susanna is crewing on *Qualistores*.'

Susanna, Chloe's other half was the soft feminine one in the partnership to Chloe's butch. He knew that Crickerman had taken Susanna on as navigator and she was a good one.

'I can't cheer,' said Josie. 'That Crickerman put my uncle out of business. He was a dairy farmer and Qualistores have forced the price of milk in store down below bottled water.'

'Yeah,' said Dave. 'That all fits with everything I've heard.'

'At least Crickerman skippers his own yacht,' Josie had to admit. 'Whoever is the boss of that Swiss outfit; he's nowhere near his boat.'

Just after dawn the next morning they stood and watched as *Qualistores* took the winning gun on the finish line. The sleek sixty five foot maxi yacht was an impressive sight as with all sail set she passed up the Sound to the yacht harbour for wild celebration and spilt Champagne. The dapper Hengist Crickerman made a suitably modest speech to the TV cameras and the crew departed to celebrate in their own fashion. Other finishers appeared out of the light April mist until finally *Avocet Computers* came in fifth. She sailed over the finish line as required; though her sail area was reduced to a storm trysail and a large genoa jib.

'Looks like she's lost her main,' said Dave. 'Can't think why; it's been less than force five the last few days.' By now he and Josie stood alone. Chloe had gone to find Susanna.

An hour later Dave saw Alfred Ollavasen as he stood on the pontoon beside his yacht. He approached the man gently. *Avocet* had made the pace throughout the double crossing and was the strong favourite. It was unlikely that Ollavasen would be best pleased to see a journalist. Still wearing his sea going orange dry suit the man was a tall, muscular, fair-haired, bearded Dane. He was far less depressed than Dave had expected. 'Mainsail been getting weaker all trip,' he shrugged his shoulders. 'So what, you lose some you win some. We much better next time.'

Dave put away his pocket recorder and turned towards the shore. 'Could do with another drink,' he muttered. He and Josie reached the roadside and turned towards the yacht club.

For twenty three-years-old Josie life was good. She too was a writer and a journalist and she had found this wonderful man. He was tall, muscular and fit, with shoulder length blond hair startling blue eyes and a gentleness and humour that belied his classic good looks and antipodes accent. Dave was a Kiwi from New Zealand a land she had never visited. Dave had promised to take her there next Christmas away from the cold and rain of London. How she adored this man even if he did work for the scurrilous Daily Banner. Dave was everything that Josie fantasised about in a man: his looks, blond haired, with  the strength of a racing yachtsman and the build of a rugby player. Dave had been both of these but had never reached the peak in either. He would laugh about this. "Them as can do and them as can't write about it". Yes, Dave had a sense of humour and patience and consideration that gave their love making an intensity that sometimes made her think her head would explode with pleasure. Josie had found Dave, she loved him and she would fight to keep him.

Dave wrote about sailing for a dozen magazines and papers. For the Banner he had to broaden his field.  Sailing could never be a spectator sport. As Dave said there might be five million recreational sailors in the UK, but opposed to that were the fifty five million who couldn't tell one end of a boat from another. As a Kiwi, Dave knew his rugby; he had a fair knowledge of cricket, tennis and athletics, while he was already immersed in the tangled politics of the English Premier League.

Josie was also a writer. She had worked on two local sheets in outer London and six months ago her debut romantic novel, *Eloise's Lover,* had been accepted by a publisher. Although the romance set in the past had strong echoes of her own love life, her success was a big milestone and along with Dave's rising earnings her own publisher's advance had enabled them to furnish and make comfortable their little Bayswater apartment. Would they marry? Oh if only, but Dave had dropped hints about tying the knot in New Zealand. Could she then have a baby just like these friends of Dave whom she had yet to meet?

Josie had walked outside the yacht club lounge to light her cigarette; she would have to break this habit if she was to have children. It was a gloomy evening with a darkened sky spitting with rain. A young man was standing in the shadows and immediately she felt a pang of nervousness. He moved rather furtively into the light.

'Please, Miss. I need to talk to David Manning. It's sorta' urgent but it's confidential.'

'He's in there,' she replied. The man seemed harmless enough. He was clearly a yachtsman. He was dressed in jeans and jumper but his brown hair was tousled and his face and hands deeply suntanned.

'It's a bit too public in there. I need to talk in confidence and I want to show him something. It's dirty tricks but I don't want my name associated.'

***CHAPTER 3***

'There is something wrong here. It just couldn't happen. You know what I think?' Steve turned away from his computer and stared at Kirsten.

'No, I don't know what you think and if you go on throwing these tantrums you'll have another stroke.' Kirsten was getting bored with her husband's obsession. She was worried too. She was the chair of Easterbroke sails and this failure of one of their mainsails in top competition was not going to help their marketing at a time when there was a faint glow of economic recovery. Of course for Steve it was worse. His expertise was called in question. A racing mainsail that he had designed and tested had failed in a major yacht race. Steve had raged around their Chichester sail loft all week and had found nothing that would explain this happening. The loyal staff had tolerated this as they were all happy that the fault did not lie with them.

'Yes, you know what I think. It's sabotage.'

'Oh, come on, Steve. This isn't Olifa and Garcia. There's no gambling involved so who gains?'

'That I don't know, but if I'm right someone will pay for it.'

Kirsten started as there sounded a tap on the window. She could see the face of her son-in-law, Tom and behind him Emily with a well wrapped little bundle.

Kirsten let out a laugh of delight and ran to the front door. 'Oh come in you two it's far too cold for little Peter to be out there.'

Dave led the way down the road until they came to an empty bus shelter. Josie and the stranger followed. It was starting to rain in earnest now with gusts of cold wind off the harbour. Dave cast around for some cover and led the way inside the shelter.

'Shouldn't be overheard in here,' said Dave. 'Right, what's this about?'

'I don't want to give my name and what I've got to say is off the record.'

'I do need to know who I'm talking to,' said Dave. This man certainly looked the part. His arms beneath the T-shirt bulged with muscle and the hands and face had the real suntan of a seaman. Dave was still not certain if he was dealing with a sane member of the public or someone with a delusional persecution complex. It was surprising how many of the latter were involved in competitive sport.

'All right, I'm Ed.'

'Ed who?'

'Just Ed for now.'

'All right, Ed. Have you some connection with sport or sailing, because that's my line of country.'

'I'm a professional offshore crewman. Look, I need to cover my back. I live for sailing and I don't want to be excluded for ever.'

'Why should that be?'

'Because there's been some dirty work in that Atlantic race. It's something I overheard. Didn't take much notice at the time.'

'Go on.'

'Hengist Crickerman offered Ollavasen half a million US dollars to throw that race.'

Dave was becoming irritated. It looked as if he was dealing with a nutter after all. 'Why the hell should he do that?'

'Because he likes winning.'

'Well, so do we all but we don't bribe the opposition. This is sailing for God's sake not Italian football.'

'Ok – Ok, listen – I'll come clean. Before the race I was at the briefing session here in Plymouth. We had all the skippers and crews there. When it finished I went for a walk. How I wish I hadn't. Then I saw Hengist and Ollavasen. They seemed to be arguing about something. I went over to speak to them but they clammed up and completely ignored me. I wasn't pleased in fact I was bloody insulted. I was one of Hengist's crewmen and Ollavasen is a shithouse. So, I walked round the corner and then I thought, sod you Hengist, I will make you acknowledge me. So I turned round and then I heard them. They couldn't see me but I could just make them out through the hedge I was behind.

'I heard Ollavasen say, "I can't do that – it's not fair on Steve Simpson". Then Hengist says "all right we'll up that to half a million in US dollars. Alfred, I want that race". That was it,'

Dave looked at the man. Yes, he might be mad but he genuinely believed what he had told them. 'Thank you, Ed. I'll not write anything about this yet until I've made my own enquiries.'

'Mr Manning, I told you, I don't like Ollavasen. He tried to rape Sammy, my girl, until she scratched his face. I might just fix him myself. I'd enjoy that.'

'When was this?'

'In Copenhagen by one of the yacht clubs. Sammy's brother saved her. Bastard, Ollavasen seemed to think he could have any girl on his home ground.'

Dave beckoned to Josie and they walked away leaving the man Ed in something of a trance.

'Wow,' said Josie. 'What do you make of all that? Was he telling the truth about a rape and who is this Steve whatnot that the man mentioned?'

'He was referring to Sir Stephen Simpson, double Olympic gold, top sail maker and a very big wheel in the sailing world. Good guy too. He's the father of Emily who we were talking about.' Dave walked on a few paces. 'I don't like the sound of this sexual assault, but the bribery allegation sounds pretty unlikely and that Ed has a personal grievance against Ollavasen. All the same Crickerman is a guy who likes winning and may not be too fussy about how he does it.'

Josie was puzzled. 'I still don't get it. There were nine entries in that race surely Crickerman couldn't bribe all of them?'

'He didn't have to. *Avocet* was the scratch boat and the best crew. Everyone knew that once she moved into the lead then race over.'

Dave could smell a hot story and one that would delight the Daily Banner. Hengist Crickerman was not flavour of the month with the Banner. The over-flamboyant Australian billionaire was ruthless with developing his retail empire. Nobody had ever proved anything, but rumours and whispers said the man had ways of smoothing his path with not only local planners but even as far as Westminster. Digging by the Banner last year had revealed that the major political parties had all received funds indirectly from Crickerman. Dave had phoned the Banner's editor as soon as he had finished with the crewman, Ed. He had been given enthusiastic support and a good lump sum of expenses.

Dave had done some checking. The man he had spoken to was Edwin Coulden a professional yacht crewman who had worked around boatyards and sail makers. It was interesting that the man had never lasted very long in any job he'd held. More significant Coulden had been in trouble with the law. He had been fined for a violent assault on a traffic warden. Dave didn't know the circumstances and anyway he had been sorely tempted himself, more than once, to thump one of those officious bastards. More significant to Dave was Coulden's admission that he had a personal grudge against Ollavasen; some fight over a girl. He needed to discover more.

Josie had gone off with some girl friends shopping in town leaving Dave to entertain three of *Avocet's* crew to a Chinese meal at the Wet Wok restaurant on the Plymouth waterfront. The overnight rain had passed over. It was warm, one of the first hot days of the year and they were able to enjoy their food on an outside table. The crew men were typical of their sort: athletic build, muscles bulging, tanned faces and bleached hair. Dave watched with amusement as the three wolfed down their loaded plates of sweet and sour and all the other delicacies. Dave needed to introduce the subject of the Atlantic race and tactfully extract such information as he could. The crewmen were cheerful laid back guys and Dave guessed fine seamen if not mentally the sharpest tools in the box.

'Yeah, it was weird,' said one. 'That main was Kevlar and that's supposed to be bullet proof or something – isn't it?'

'That's right,' said his friend. 'Indestructible is what I was told.'

'Seems it wasn't though,' said Dave. 'What about sunlight? I'm told Kevlar doesn't like it.'

'UV damage never! This is North Atlantic – cold and wet all trip. That's what's so weird,' said the first speaker. 'We almost had land in sight and the wind's dropping so Alf orders we take out the reefs and set full main.'

'What happened then?' asked Dave.

'The whole bloody thing imploded,' said the third crewman. 'I was acting as mainsheet trimmer. The batten shot out and then it just fell apart with a great rip along one seam. Skipper had no choice; take the whole thing off and set that stupid little tri-sail.

Dave was not convinced. The tri-sail was an emergency tiny triangle of heavy fabric for setting in force ten or above. Dave had sailed as a crewman with a New Zealand
round-the-world yacht. He would have improvised something with one of the larger jibs, or why bother with a main when in a light fair wind they could crack up the largest spinnaker. He would have done had he been serious about finishing the race.

He hadn't enough yet to write anything; he needed more background. He found Qualistores the company on the internet but learned little. The company preceded by some years the takeover by Hengist Crickerman. Crickerman had brought in huge capital resources but it was not clear where he had obtained most of this wealth. Hengist had been born in Melbourne the son of a German refugee teacher. He had left school at seventeen and started dealing in car parts. At twenty three he had married the heiress of Qualistore then a chain of small shops sited in and around Melbourne. Whether the wife's family had approved of Hengist was not clear. But the man had prospered with the aid of a partnership with a Singapore business man. By the 1980s Hengist had acquired shops in Argentina, Chile and then a small retail chain in Texas. All these businesses had been renamed Qualistores. In 1990 Hengist Crickerman had bought a major retail chain in the UK to add to his empire which by now was worldwide with its HQ in London. Dave could remember the first Qualistore branches opening in three districts of Auckland.

It seemed that sailing had been an early interest of Hengist's and he was good at it, the racing side anyway. Dave suspected that Hengist needed to win and had the supreme self-confidence to do so more often than not. A *Qualistores* yacht had been among the front runners in the Sydney Hobart race and now Hengist Crickerman had joined the European circuit and Dave guessed that now the man needed to win more than ever.

Alfred Ollavasen shot a covert glance around the dockside. It was dark now except for the glow of a single floodlight. He bent down and humped the heavy sail bag onto his shoulders. He had just this one final task; get rid of the evidence. He should feel guilty but no. These were desperate times and he was entitled to his burning resentment. His business his home; his whole life was at stake and that Swiss bastard had refused to help with a single extra dollar. Well bad on him. Now it needed Crickerman to pay up as he had promised and he had better come good. Alfred could understand Crickerman not wishing to deal with him direct but who was this Garcia and why did he only want to deal via that nasty little girl? He half carried and half dragged the bulky object, loaded it into the rear of the pickup and headed for the landfill site. He never noticed the black Volvo that pulled out of the yacht club car park and then trailed him at a discreet distance.

# CHAPTER 5

'Can't see the point of that,' said Tom. 'Baby onboard.' He was glaring at the sticker in the rear window of Emily's Nissan. 'I mean who cares, us apart?'

'It's a warning,' said Emily. 'It means back-off tailgater.'

'Some hope that. How is your dad today?'

'Bear with a sore head,' she replied.

'Oh yeah. I thought barristers weren't supposed to talk in cliché.'

Emily laughed. 'You clearly haven't sat in many courtrooms.' She reached inside the car door picked up the baby and handed him to Tom. 'Pete, go to daddy.'

Tom looked at the little face emerging from the wrappings. 'He's Peter not Pete. You'll turn him into a yobbo.'

'We'll see. Right now he needs a feed.'

They reached the warmth of the cottage and Emily whisked Peter away from Tom and unlatched her top. Personally he would rather she fed the baby in the privacy of the downstairs bathroom. Tom wasn't too pleased with this facility. He felt upstairs was the place for bathing. It was expecting too much for Emily to hide herself away from him while she breast fed the kiddy. At least Emily was keeping covered and decent in the garden. The nudism at her parent's home was the one part of her Scandinavian ethos that had alienated him since the earliest days of their relationship five years ago.

Tom felt desperately sorry for his father-in-law, Steve. That whole thing about a failed mainsail just didn't make sense. The fabric with which it was made was Kevlar and that was indestructible. Couldn't *Avocet's* crew have cut away the damaged part and reset the sail as a reef. The shots he had seen on TV showed the boat carrying an emergency trysail. That just didn't make sense in a failing breeze. Steve was mumbling about conspiracy but Tom was wary. He had had quite enough of dirty tricks during the Olifa Olympics and that Garcia. And after all there was no gambling involved with this two leg Atlantic race; just a whole lot of billionaires waving their cheque books.

'Nappies,' called Emily. 'Come on, modern man – your turn.'

'You'll have to show me again.'

'All right, once more – but you'll be on your own after midnight. I need sleep.'

'I'm not standing for this,' Steve yelled. 'Not available. I'll give them not available!'

'All right, will you calm down,' said Kirsten. 'I've told you before if you go on like this all you'll get is another stroke.' This time they were in the office at Easterbroke Sails. Steve had been reading the morning emails and he was not pleased.

'Right, that's it,' Steve fumed. 'I'll ring that solicitor, what's his name…'

'And tell him what?'

'That we've had a sail deliberately nobbled and it's costing us reputation.'

'Let's see that email,' said Kirsten as she peered over his shoulder.

*Regret damaged sail is unavailable for inspection.*

'They're hiding something. We've a legal right…'

'Tell you what,' said Kirsten in that irritating, soothing voice that Steve remembered from his sick bed days. 'I'll contact Cousin Alfred and see what he has to say.'

This did not please Steve either. Alfred Ollavasen was a very distant cousin of Kirsten's who had appeared out of the woodwork. Steve thought him an ill-mannered surly Dane. He had not been pleased to discover that Ollavasen had been in serious trouble with the Danish police over a rape allegation.

'Yes, you do that. But I'm still talking to the solicitor. Who is this bloke who owns *Avocet?* "

'I know that,' said Kirsten. 'Swiss computer giant: Erich Shilltinberg, eleventh richest man in the world or something like that.'

'I've found it,' said Dave. 'It's a bloody great lump.' He pointed to his car. 'There, I've roped it to my dinghy trailer.'

'Have you looked at it?' asked Keith.

'No, I need to find somewhere off-road that's quiet and you can take the pics.'

Dave had rung Keith on his mobile. Keith was a freelance photographer who worked the sailing scene. Fortunately Keith had heard the undercurrents of rumour already.

'They can't say that you've nicked it can they?' Keith sounded alarmed.

'No, they can't. That thickhead Dane left it in a landfill site.'

'How did you come by it?'

'That's the odd thing. I had a tip off from someone on my mobile earlier today.'

'Who was that?'

'Some bloke, spoke with a bit of a foreign accent, could have been another Dane. I've no idea who he was, but it's the kind of thing that happens in my business. Sometimes it's a windup, but this time we're spot on.'

'Ollavasen wasn't very clever if he let someone know what he was up to and why just leave it lying in a tip?'

'I dunno'; I suppose if it's Kevlar it wouldn't burn well anyway.'

Dave found the car park near the edge of Bodmin Moor and stopped the Renault next to his dinghy trailer half-concealed behind a large thorn bush. The morning was once again wet and misty and in this early season. Apart from one seemingly abandoned van, no other cars or people could be seen. Dave and Keith undid the ties that held the awkward cylindrical bag to the trailer.

'How did Ollavasen get this to the dump?' asked Keith.

'He's got a pick up truck. He's a strong armed bastard so I suppose he didn't find handling it such a strain.'

With some sweat and effort they slid the sail out of its cover. 'Let's have a look,' said Dave. Slowly they unrolled the sail until he saw the ripped seam.

'Batten pockets' empty,' he said as he looked closer. 'Oh my God, get your camera, Keith. Look at that. It's been spiked, no doubt whatever.'

Back in his hotel Dave emailed the editor of the Daily Banner. Within ten minutes the reply came.

*Good work. Write the story.*

So that was it. If the Banner was prepared to take on the likes of Crickerman and the more obscure Erich Shilltinberg, then the editor must know something that Dave did not.

None-the-less he had better be a mite cryptic in his accusations.

'Em, come look at this,' Tom called.

'Hang on, I'm still feeding Peter.'

'When you're both ready, but I've just had this email from Dave and it's a bit odd.'

Five minutes later Emily was there leaning over his shoulder. He caught the scent of her perfume and felt her soft hand as she touched his face. How lucky he was, how lucky that he had found this beautiful, talented, girl and persuaded her to marry him. And now they were complete with their little son.

*David Manning*
*To Tom & Emily Stoneman.*
*CC Chloe Te Koote.*


*Hi you guys,*
*Congratulations on the new arrival. Hope you are all three doing well.*
*I think you will be interested in tomorrow's Daily Banner. Big article page 2.*
*Tell Emily's Dad as well – he'll appreciate it.*

*Hope we'll see you back on the water again soon.*
*Josie sends her love.*
*Take care,*
*Dave.*


'I'm not sure my Dad'll want to buy the Banner,' said Emily.

'I wouldn't want to normally,' said Tom. 'But this must be a sailing story that Dave's written.'

'It may be something to do with the Trans Atlantic two-leg,' said Emily. 'I bet it involves that Crickerman. You know there's an out of town Qualistores opening next year just down by the big roundabout. I think I'll try it out.'

'I guess we'll save a bit of cash if you do. Anyway they say Crickerman's a good sailor.'

'Dad thinks he's a cheat.'


Alfred Ollavasen had not been paid and he was nervous, frustrated and angry. He had heard nothing from his contact, the little girl with the irritating voice. The business man, Garcia, had agreed to pay the half a million dollars into an offshore account. The girl would then give Alfred the account details and passwords.

All this was supposed to happen within forty eight hours of *Avocet* crossing the finish. He didn't know the girl's name she was an enigma. Alfred wondered what would happen if the truth came out.

He doubted if the law in either England or Denmark would take much notice. There was no gambling involved just a plot to enlarge Crickerman's ego. Alfred needed that money if he was to survive. But if Crickerman defaulted on their agreement well the world would know the truth.

Once again he rang Crickerman on his mobile. No reply; just a stupid voice telling him to leave a message.

'Ok, I leave you bloody message. You pay up or I tell the world that you are fucking scoundrel.'

## CHAPTER 6

The weeks went by surprisingly quickly. The baby kept Emily and
Tom active through twenty four hours but not excessively. Peter was
weaned off breast milk and persuaded with some difficulty to accept a
bottle. This of course meant Tom being drawn into the feeding side as
soon as he came home from work. Emily seemed to be thriving on her
child rearing and had avoided any serious post natal depression. In
fact she had hinted to Tom. 'I'd rather like a brood of kids.' For Tom
this was a mixed blessing. Child conception would mean of necessity
a return of sex, but he was far from sure he wanted his life taken over
by a household of squalling kids.

The domestic scene was broken by a phone call from Tony Travis.
'How is it all going Emily?'

'No worries we're all fine, I'm hoping to be able to go back to
work in a week or so. We've a lovely lady a few doors away who's
agreed to be nanny if I'm away more than ten hours.'

'That's good news. Emily, I've got something for you but it won't
happen before September. I would like you to junior for me in a high-
profile libel case.'

'Libel?' this had made Emily sit up and take notice. A civil action
between wealthy protagonists meant a bounty for lawyers. Her
earnings had been slim, mostly from legal aid defences. A good
payout would be very welcome.

'What's the dispute?' she asked.

Now she had a shock. 'It's that article in the Daily Banner from
last April. That's why I would like you with me. It's all about yacht
racing and you are big in that world.'

'I don't know. I haven't seen a boat in months. Not since Peter was
born anyway.'

'We've been engaged by the defence. You see the Banner
suggested that money had changed hands to throw a yacht race, but
the complainant says he can prove he never paid a cent. It's an
unusual sort of case – could go either way but the Banner are sharing
the cost with Erich Shilltenberg – do you know of him?'

Emily had to think. 'He's the owner of the yacht involved.'

'*Avocet Computers?*'

'That's the one. Why is he involved? If there really was a

conspiracy he's a wounded party.'

'Apparently the man is so incensed about the whole affair that he only wants to get back at Mr Crickerman.'

Emily now felt unease. 'Tony, that article was written by a friend of ours Dave Manning. Is he in trouble?'

'Well, I've now seen the article and it's very muted. But no, Mr Manning is not named. It's only the Daily Banner.'

'Will he lose his job?'

'I shouldn't think so. The tabloid press are very protective of their own. It could be any one of them next. As I said Mr Manning has not been intrusive in any way. Certainly no phone hacking involved.'

'Will you want me to cross examine?'

'You may well get a turn, but mostly I want you to research background. You know the South Coast boat scene better than me. None of us have forgotten the Walter Smidgin case.'

'Nor have I. Smidgin comes out of prison this year and I'm worried. He told someone in the jail that he would go looking for me.'

'Have you informed the police?'

'Tom has and they took him seriously. They say they've given the man a warning.'

This court hearing had been Emily's first defence. On the face of it a lost cause until Emily discovered that this man Smidgin had deliberately given false evidence in an attempt to convict an innocent man. That case had given Emily a huge career boost.

'Nothing is going to happen just yet,' said Travis. 'But when it does I want you to keep your ear to the ground.'


The Daily Banner article had soothed Steve's anger. The photographs of the ripped sail in particular the close ups of the severed stitching had relieved Easterbroke of blame. It had been a bad few weeks but now thank God it was over. Orders were picking up and at last with warmer weather he could go sailing again. Steve had not raced since his triumph in the Olifa Paralympics but his own little cruising yacht *Puffin* was back afloat and he and Kirsten were planning a few days away with Emily's younger brother John-Kaj as crew.

Emily with Tom and Peter had called at home regularly and Emily was able to bring her parents the news from Tony Travis. 'How exactly is this Alfred Ollavasen related to us?' she asked.

'That's a sore point,' said her father. He had never taken to this Ollavasen character. The man was a good seaman but he was a dull, morbid fellow to whom it was a struggle to make any conversation.

Apart from that there were all those ugly rumours from Denmark.

'We told you about Gerda Elgaad,' said Kirsten.

'I know that,' Emily replied. 'What I suffered because of that woman and Tom was nearly killed. I still dream about it.'

'We know. But that was all through one delusional man and he's dead. Anyway Gerda had a sister called Anna and it seems this man is Anna's great grandson.

'We've only met him once and that was before this Atlantic race.'

'I tell you why I asked,' said Emily. 'Tony wants me to go to Hamble and chat up this character. Tony thinks that me being related and a female will make the bloke open up.'

'He's a mighty dull fellow, but as you say he might open up to you. Just be careful, don't get too close. He's got an ugly reputation with women.'

Alfred Ollavasen was feeling tense and angry with a tinge of nervousness. He was standing on the pontoon at Hamble Point Marina on the west side facing the shoreline. It was dark here and that suited him. Tonight he would know if Crickerman would keep his side of the deal. This was the spot he had negotiated with the girl. Three times she had met him here and each of those times he had been disappointed. The mysterious Garcia was away on business; if the man really exists, thought Alfred. Then she said she was waiting to be told the account numbers and passwords. Alfred had had enough. Tonight he would have a result or the deal was off. As it was he faced financial ruin with nowhere to turn. He had hoped last year to leach some money out of this cousin Kirsten Simpson, or Lady Simpson, for God's sake. A Danish girl with these ridiculous English titles; it made him sick. He looked at his watch: twenty two fifteen. If Crickerman's intermediary girl didn't show up in the next few minutes then that was it. He might be ruined but he would take Crickerman down with him. Or maybe not yet. That slimy journalist Manning had something coming to him as well. The creepy little shit must have followed Alfred to the waste tip. Maybe he could let Manning and his newspaper take the rap with this libel trial. If Crickerman won then he Alfred could reveal the real truth. Who was that British politician who had gone to prison for lying under oath in a similar scam? Yes, jail that would be a pay back to Crickerman and his shopping empire.

The lights outside the main office building had suddenly gone out. It must be a power fault as he could see plenty of illumination from nearby houses. No more messing around. He strode up the ramp determined to settle this thing one way or another. He stared around him looking for his visitor. He walked to the office building and there he saw a figure standing waiting. This person was his contact or was it? Why swathe your face in a scarf and wear a woolly cap. Alfred didn't care his anxiety had aroused his inbred rage. He caught the person by the left arm. 'Where's my money?' It was the right hand that wielded the knife and plunged it into his throat and again and again. He staggered away blood streaming down and gushing from his neck and mouth until he reached the edge of the pontoon and fell into the sea.

# CHAPTER 7

Emily was surprised to see the car park at Hamble Point awash with police cars and two vans stopped among the laid up yachts. Now, what, she wondered? Theft from this marina had featured in the Smidgin case but this looked more serious than the nicking of a few outboard motors. She was even more startled to see that her way was barred by a police incident tape. A couple of uniform constables were standing there; so unabashed she marched up to them.

'What's going on?' she asked.

'Sorry Madam, but this area is banned to the public. You'll have to leave I'm afraid.'

'What's happened?'

'There has been an incident.'

'That's bloody obvious. What kind of incident?'

'Officers are investigating the scene and no doubt there will be a press statement in due course.'

Emily dug into her handbag, pulled out one of her business cards and handed it to the man who had spoken.

'Lawyer, are you?' He peered at Emily none too politely.

'Yes, I am also looking for evidence in a serious civil case and there's a man I need to speak to.'

'Who's that?'

'He's a yacht master called Alfred Ollavasen…'

'You don't say. Well, lady you're a bit late.'

'Has he gone somewhere?'

'You could say that. He's gone to meet his maker. Someone cut his throat last night.'

Emily tried to take this in but couldn't get to grips with the news. A man was walking toward the tape, and a man whom she had seen before in court: Chief-Superintendent Hollins. This very senior police officer was a man known to her apart from court work. Hollins was an impressive looking fifty something with greying hair. Evidently he was still a detective as he wore a dark suit in contrast to the uniformed police who had stopped Emily. Years ago, before she was born, this man had been involved with her Dad and Frank Matheson in that horrible business with Lindgrune the blackmailer. He had been a young ambitious detective then. Now he was a very big name in police work and his presence confirmed that this incident, so called, was a very significant one.

'Mrs Stoneman, how are you? Are you due to board a yacht because you can't today I'm afraid.'

Emily, her surprise now under control told the superintendent the reason for her arrival.

'Very well,' said Hollins. 'Mrs Stoneman if you would follow me.' He lifted the tape for Emily to pass under.

The police had sequestered an empty office as an incident room. Hollins himself made Emily a cup of tea. 'Now it's only form but can you tell me where you were last night between half past nine and eleven o'clock.'

Emily gaped. 'I didn't kill him. We needed him alive.'

'I'm sure you're right. As I say it's only form.'

Emily laughed. 'I was at Firs Farm in South Marshall at my parent's house: Sir Stephen and Lady Kirsten Simpson…'

'Of course, I remember your father.'

Emily added. 'My husband was there and my brother and if you like my baby Peter but he's only a few weeks old.'

'All right, Mrs Stoneman. I doubt we'll be checking.'

'Look, Mr Hollins. We needed Ollavasen alive. If he could have been persuaded to tell the truth then the complainant party would have been demolished. Even if you people took an interest I doubt you'd prove criminal intent.'

'Maybe not, but Mr Crickerman would certainly take a beating.'

'The judge would likely award costs against him,' Emily mused,

'With his millions he wouldn't notice. Damage his ego though.'

Emily looked at him. 'Seems you don't like Crickerman?'

'Let's just say the man interests us, for other reasons apart from this yachting fracas.'

'Mr Hollins, can you tell me anything? You're officer has already told me Ollavarsen's throat was cut.'

Hollins glared at her. 'All right Mrs Stoneman. On one condition: no talk to the media.'

'I'll have to tell my boss. He's sent me down to persuade Ollavasen to talk.'

'All right, but tell him we'll be holding a press conference this evening. At present no suspect, no clear motive…'

'What about CCTV?

'That's why we believe this was premeditated. The power was cut to the shoreside lighting and the CCTV was demobilised. Security into the building isn't that good or at least not for a real professional. The disconnection was done by someone who knew what he was doing.'

'Are you thinking in terms of a hit man?' asked Emily.

'Mrs Stoneman, that is overdramatic. We're not ruling anything in or out at this stage.'

That, thought Emily is real copper's stonewalling and the press won't like it.

Hollins escorted her back to the incident tape and lifted it for her to pass under. Like vultures attracted to a ripe prey, the press were gathering. Emily saw four men waving cameras and a woman talking in front of a TV camera. As one they tried to surround her babbling questions. She was able to rasp in her most authoritarian voice. 'I am not the police. I am here on business.'

She sighed. It was a lovely late June morning, the sun was warm, the sky blue. It was high water and yachts and small craft were moving in and out of the Hamble. Emily walked back to the car. She was the bearer of bad news and suddenly she only wanted to be home with her baby.

Emily found there was no escape. Of course she had been recognised and the Travis chambers had been bombarded with calls from national and the local media. The press and television were determined to connect the murder with the libel case. Emily had hardly arrived home and walked through the door when she was greeted by Lily Lorrimer, Peter's nanny. 'Emily, there's messages on your answerphone, all about a murder,' the girl's voice dropped to a morbid whisper.

'Don't answer them,' said Emily. 'I don't think I will either.' She gave Lily a brief explanation. 'Anyway how is Peter?'

'He's asleep. You've got a good one there; eats and sleeps, not like my one when she was that age.'

Superintendent Hollins, watched as Emily left the marina. The young lawyer's information was most interesting. It also looked as if this investigation was going to be mired in politics. Hengist Crickerman, if he was involved, might to be too big a fish for the police to touch and was that galling. Crickerman was known to be a ruthless entrepreneur and there was evidence that he had cooperated with mafia style rings and used intimidation. But these suspicions were all confined to the third world or Eastern Europe. Hollins didn't care for Qualistores although his wife and daughters insisted in doing their weekly shopping there. *"A penny saved is another to spend..."* That was

Qualistores irritating TV slogan. From what he'd seen of Margaret's shopping list that slogan was a fraud in itself.

Hollins had no love for brash Australians, but he'd better be careful. Meeting young Emily had reminded him of that detective in Sussex, what was his name? God I must be getting old, he muttered to himself. Emily had once been that little abducted kid whose rescue had been a sensation. That investigation had been hindered by a detective suffering from strain and overwork. Yes, Le Bois, Inspector le Bois, that was the man. His prejudice had led him to delusion and finally full madness and death. No, if he wanted to become a chief constable he must play this one by the book. Anyway it wasn't his investigation. It belonged to area CID and Detective Chief Inspector Garry Marchway. Garry was already down there on the dock with a forensic team. No he wasn't, he was walking towards the office carrying a cardboard box.

'Hello, Garry, you look pleased.'

'Maybe, sir, I don't know yet but we've found these CCTV tapes from a month or so back and they show Ollavasen chatting to a weedy looking girl.'

'A month back. Could be one of his fancy bits.'

'I don't think so, sir. There's something about the body language and we've found three similar incidents. Ollavasen doesn't look happy and the girl looks scared of him.'

'With that man's reputation she'd have good reason to be nervous.'

'What are you going to do with them?'

'I'm having them computer enhanced and then we'll seriously think about showing the result to the public, maybe on the next Crimewatch.'

'We'd better give the girl a chance to come forward first.'

'Yes, sir, that's implicit in the way we handle this. We'll publish the blurred images first and see what happens.'

### *CHAPTER 8*

Dave Manning and his girl friend Josie were in Scotland when the phone call came.

They were sailing their dinghy in an event off the coast of Argyle when the irritating ring tone sounded from the inside of Dave's dry suit.

'Sod that, I'm not stopping for whoever.'

'I think you should,' said Josie. 'It might be important.' She helped him unwind the suit zip fastener.

Dave grumbled, but with a struggle dug out the phone. 'Hello…'

It was the editor of the Banner. 'Dave, get to Southampton. Your man's been murdered.'

Feeding frenzy might be a cliché but it fitted the media response to the killing of Alfred Ollavasen.

YACHT HERO STABBED …CONTRACT KILLING RUMOUR…DID SKIPPER THROW HIS RACE…POLICE SAY NO ARRESTS SOON.

Dave was amazed, he had never in his lifetime known a sailing related story that had driven politics, the economy and the Middle East off the front pages. Of course it was not the yacht element that was feeding this. It was the big names: Crickerman and Shilltinberg and the possibility that these billionaires might have had a dirty hand in the business. Of course no one dared to voice these names openly.

Dave had been forced to abandon his dinghy race, then whisk the boat onto the trailer and take the road south. He had arrived in Hamble ten hours later to take over from a Banner reporter, a young girl with zero knowledge of boats let alone offshore racing. Dave set to and busied himself interviewing marina workers and irritated yacht owners who were still denied access to their pontoons. Frankly he couldn't extract any more information than had already been gathered by the young reporter. Ollavasen's crew had dispersed and the Atlantic race organisers would only release contact details to the police.

It was Emily Stoneman who made the only useful suggestion when he called her at home on the first evening. 'Can't tell you anything

34

more than you know already,' she said. 'You're the only bloody reporter I'm prepared to talk with.'

'I know, I'm sorry but I think I'm the only writer who can bring some sanity to all this.'

'Ok, come over to dinner tomorrow evening, Chloe's going to be here with that girl friend of hers. She's Susanna the one who navigated for Crickerman.'

Dave then concentrated on whatever he could discover about Ollavasen's private life. The Simpson family had reported him to be a dull fellow however good his sailing skills. The man was unmarried and seemingly dedicated to his career as a yacht skipper, but then Dave began to pick up fresh rumours. If Ollavasen was a bachelor he was definitely not a gay one. The rugged looking Dane had never been short of female company although none of these relationships had lasted long. A Danish colleague of Dave's had told him that Ollavasen's approach to women and been direct and to the point. Sex for Alfred had apparently been a case of blunt, brutal and short. This had resulted in an assault charge that had nearly ended with the man in jail. Eventually he had been ordered to pay a huge sum in damages to the luckless victim. Ollavasen's home had been seized and his yacht chandlery business had collapsed. No wonder the man had swallowed his pride and taken part in this alleged race throwing scam. But Alfred had still been numbered among the world's top offshore sailors and that was probably the reason why Erich Shilltinberg had still trusted him to skipper *Avocet Computers*.

Even as they arrived at the Stoneman house Josie could hear Chloe's voice. Chloe, Dave's fellow countrywoman was a good friend even though she had a presence that dominated any situation or place. Dave walked up to her gave her a hug and Chloe introduced them to her partner Susanna. Susanna was the feminine one of the pair: petite, blonde, with deeply tanned face and shoulders. So this was the navigator girl on *Qualistores*. Emily came into the room carrying her baby and for a few moments she let Josie hold the little boy. It was lovely but the experience only made her feel envious and increasingly broody. Maybe one day?

'Tom's been in Winchester and he's got a copy of the *Echo*,' said Emily. 'They've released some pictures but I don't know that they'll be much use.

IS THIS THE YACHT MUDERER

The pictures were grainy but they did reveal a man who looked very much like the rugged Dane seemingly talking to a smaller and more obscured figure.

'It says that picture was from a tape in late April,' said Tom. 'Could be almost anybody.'

'The police want the girl, if it is a girl to come forward and be eliminated,' said Emily.

'But it's such poor res,' said Josie as she read the paper. 'And the body language is odd. I would say Ollavasen is threatening the girl and she's nervous and backing off.'

'Yes,' said Tom. 'That squares with everything we know about Ollavasen with women.'

'The Banner will be making a meal of this in tomorrow's edition,' Dave commented.

'Darling,' said Josie, with her arm around him. 'Do you have to work for that crowd?' It was the question she had asked before and it always had the same answer.

'Oh they're not so bad and anyway we need the cash.'

That was certainly true. Josie's book sales were steady and her freelance work regular. But they needed the Banner's retainer fees as well as Dave's earnings from sailing mags.

'At least they're being good about the libel case,' said Dave. 'They've told me I won't be taking any rap if it goes sour.'

'I guess they've sold a few extra copies on the strength of all this,' Tom ginned.

'Better than that,' said Dave. 'Editor's told me that if I can come up with any more good info, I'll get a fat bonus.'

Josie turned to Susanna. 'How was life on *Qualistores*?'

'Yeah, it was great – very smooth trip.'

The girl had been a bit detached from the gathering and Josie felt sorry for her. She was such a pretty little thing; it seemed a bit of a waste. Josie notice that Susanna had taken to following Emily around offering to help with household chores. Emily treated this with cheerful tolerance. When Susie fixed a minor electrical fault in Emily's kitchen, Emily had treated the girl rather as if she was patronising a clever child.

'Yeah,' said Susanna, 'everyone's down on Hengist because he's rich, but he seemed a fair bloke to us crew.'

Josie felt a pang of guilt. This poor little girl was an odd one out in this nearly all male gathering and that included Chloe. Emily was absorbed with little Peter and in spite of Susanna's attention she tended to treat her as another child. 'You're a navigator?' Josie asked.

'Yeah, but it's no big deal nowadays – got satellite and electronics but you need the old skills if the power fails.'

'How did you get on with the rest of the crew?'

'They're all right.'

Josie gave up. Susanna seemed a dull girl in spite of a relationship with the ebullient Chloe. It must be difficult for her to be in this company and especially with Emily who was a lawyer opposing Crickerman in court. She was trusting Dave to question Tom in private and that was hard in the midst of a social gathering.

'Tell you something,' said Susanna. 'We've had a bit of a bonus. Hengist's given me and Chloe two hundred pounds of free shopping in Qualistores.'

Tom appeared wearing a kitchen apron. 'Everyone, dinner is served. I have for you a choice of five delicious curry dishes.'

'You have a concealed talent,' said Josie.

'No he hasn't,' said Emily. 'All he did was drive the car from the takeaway.'

Tom had at least managed to keep the dishes warm and in the end it was a good convivial meal. It was when they had retired to the lounge for coffee that the shock came. The television was on showing the local southern news.

'Now,' said the presenter. 'The Hamble murder. The police have issued this photo-fit of a woman they wish to speak to.'

Emily expelled a gasp of near horror. Tom sat up as if he had had an electric shock. Dave seemed almost mesmerised. He and Tom glanced at each other. 'My God,' said Tom. It's her – or is it?'

'It's only an artist's drawing,' Emily whispered. 'But it could be.'

'Who, for God's sake you people,' said Chloe. 'Who is it?'

'She once tried to kill me,' said Tom so quietly that Josie had to strain to hear him.

# CHAPTER 9

'Dione, get in here,' Hengist Crickerman called into his internal phone.

His PA appeared seconds later. Hengist was not in the best of tempers but his abrupt manner never seemed to upset Dione. Anyway she was a good Aussie and he paid her well.

'Seems like we've a sort a' royal visit,' he said.

'You mean that policeman?'

'That's the one: Chief Superintendent Hollins a very big dick from the South Coast.'

'Sure thing. How do we handle him?'

'Oh that. We will all be amazingly polite and helpful.'

'Do you think he's wise to any of this?'

'Shouldn't think so. Look I've dealt with thick dicks back home. They don't frighten me.'

'Do you want me to listen and take notes?'

'No don't bother. Now, June sales figures for our Manchester branches.'

Chief Superintendent Chris Hollins had speeded up the A3 and from there into central London. It was so easy in his official car and with a driver who knew exactly where he was bound. In this case an office block near Canary Wharf. Despite Hengist Crickerman's disdain Hollins was not an average copper. He was a high-flyer selected at an early stage for promotion. A public schoolboy and a university graduate he had been ambitious and at pains to allay any prejudice against him among his officers. In the end they liked him. He got things done. He persuaded the police authority to authorise the purchase of modern equipment and had skilfully steered his force through the times of austerity.

Qualistores head office had an executive's car park but it was full. 'Don't worry, sir,' said his driver. 'I'll park round the corner in the Daily Banner. They won't complain – they daren't.'

Hollins smoothed his uniform, put on his cap and marched into reception.

'Terrible business,' Crickerman shook his head. 'Fine fellow, great seaman – we'll all miss him.' He signalled to Dione who handed the superintendent a cup of coffee and a biscuit. Hollins saw the girl make a grimace behind her employer's back following that last comment.

'Thank you,' said Hollins. He was covertly sizing up the man opposite. Crickerman was very Australian: no formal office suit, but casual designer slacks and fawn coloured jacket, white shirt and no tie. The man was well built with sharp facial features and thinning blond hair.

'I gather you've a suspect on the run,' said Hengist. 'I don't know her – never seen her, but of course I'll help you in any way I can.'

'We are a bit concerned about this run in you are having with the Daily Banner.'

Hengist threw back his head and laughed. 'My next door neighbours. Sensationalism sells papers and they've had a hard time financially, but that's all down to poor management, apart from mucking with celebs phones. Chances are I may buy them out.'

Hollins permitted himself a smile. 'If so they won't be able to say rude things about you, sir.'

'Too right, mate.'

Hollins found it hard to dislike this man. He knew that beneath the hearty Aussie act was a very shrewd business mind. But he did have a likeable quality and Hollins knew the man's yacht crew almost worshipped him. 'However we would like to know if there is any substance in the Banner's allegations. You see Mr Crickerman, you won't have broken any laws.'

'And I can prove I haven't paid a cent to poor old Alfred. He ballsed up and lost his mainsail. Why the hell didn't he set his spinny and coast in the last two hundred miles. That's what I'd've done. But he didn't and it was me as won that.' Hengist pointed to the silver trophy in a glass case in the corner of the office.

'The Banner says the sail was nobbled.'

'More like it was a fault at the makers. That's Easterbroke and Sir bloody Steve Simpson. Why don't you talk to him?'

'Mr Crickerman, I think we already have.'

'And you police have probably been swept away by his lad-di-dah title. In our country we stopped that kinda' shit years ago.'

'You have a different outlook, sir. We British like our traditions, but you are wrong if you think a title would influence us, because it doesn't and never will.' Hollins felt he was being led in circles. It was his turn to be awkward. 'It's only a matter of form, sir, but could you tell me where you were on the night in question.'

'Yah,' Crickerman laughed. 'Thought that was coming; I have an alibi. You've got no need to go further than *the Daily Telegraph.* I was at the Lord Mayors reception for young entrepreneurs and the paper's got a picture to prove it.

'Sir we are very aware of that, but where did you go when the reception finishes?'

'Ask my lovely Dione. I went back to her flat in the building here and we had a restful night beneath the duvet. Or it wasn't that restful.'

'Thank you, sir. If we need to know more we'll be in touch.'
Superintendent Hollins left the building and found his car and driver. The latter was seated in an upmarket café that Hollins knew was frequented by staff from the Banner.

'Did you learn anything?' he asked the man.

'I'm not sure, sir, but two of them were on about our suspect. Seems she's done work for them.' He laughed. 'That old Sid Everett came in, although he's retired now.'

'We all remember him.'

'Yes, sir. I asked him if he'd ever hacked a phone. He went all shifty and said; "might've".'

Hollins settled in his seat as the car headed for the M25. It had been a most interesting morning. Yes, Hengist Crickerman had certainly been present at the Lord Mayor's reception, but he hadn't left there for the bed of the lovely Dione. The MET had already confirmed that Crickerman had ordered his private helicopter to be warmed up and ready at City Airport. The machine, with Crickerman aboard, had taken off with the pilot leaving no flight plan. Takeoff had been at nine fifteen. The helicopter had returned at six am the following morning flown by the lone pilot and without a passenger. No one seemed to know where it had landed in between but he was going to find that out.

Early next morning Dave Manning rang the London office of the Banner and spoke to the chief crime reporter. 'That's right, she's done some work for us freelance, but we haven't heard or seen sight of the bitch for months – not since last year actually. She wrote a rubbish piece about the Olifa Olympics for the *Daily Postman* that lost'em some readers.'

'Do you think the photo-fit is her?'

'I guess they've based it on the CCTV images. If we could only computer enhance the originals. But we can't from these pics the law have given us; they're rubbish.'

'Is it her? My friends think it's her.'

'As I say I'd rather see the enhanced CCTV pics. But Dave, tell you something. Your police chief from Hampshire called on Hengist Crickerman yesterday morning.'

'Well, I hope he gave the bastard a grilling.'

Next Dave rang Tom. 'How is Emily taking this?'

'Not well. She's scared that woman may try to harm Peter.'

'She really thinks it is the same one?'

'I'm not totally convinced myself, but you know Emily,' Tom sounded gloomy. 'We've rung the police and they are helpful but there's no sign out there.'

'I only met her that once in Olifa.'

'Michelle Le Bois?'

'That's the one.'

*Puffin* cleared the Chichester Harbour entrance and set course westward. It was a perfect late June day with a good seabreeze. The sun, almost too hot ashore, was  pleasantly warmth out here. This, thought Steve, was the reward for all those long months of winter ice and snow. Kirsten steered the little yacht; Steve with their son John-Kaj manned the jib sheets as they worked to windward. *Puffin* was the family's only boat now. She was a Hunter 27, a well seasoned design and some fifteen years old. This was an easily handled boat for a family of three like themselves for weekend sailing, while Tom and Emily sometimes took her for longer cruises.

'Dad, can we go look at the Super Yachts,' asked Johnnie. 'We saw them on telly last night. They're all at Gunwharf Quay.'

'Good idea,' Steve replied. 'Let's do that.'

'Will that *Avocet* be there?' asked Kirsten.

'All nine of them are there,' said Steve. Mention of *Avocet* had brought him home to events on land. Suddenly the sun didn't seem so warm. He glanced at Kirsten and she grimaced. The telepathy between them was as strong as ever.

'They must have a different skipper,' said Johnny 'The regular one's been topped.'

'Don't be flippant,' his mother snapped. 'You should show a bit of respect – Alfred was a cousin of ours and he was brutally murdered.'

'By that Michelle?'

'You should be careful what you say. Your sister's very distressed and that's bad for the little baby.'

They were approaching the two forts that guarded the Portsmouth entrance. 'There's the Spinnaker Tower,' Steve pointed. 'What a great navigational mark they've given us. You can see it from almost anywhere in the Solent.'

'We went up it last year,' said Johnny. 'Emily's friend Erin took us, but it was raining; couldn't see much except the Pompey waterfront.'

They sailed on past the forts and the Southsea shoreline until the time came to square up and enter harbour along the designated small boat channel on the West side. Now they could see the nine magnificent maxi yachts rafted together. Even to Steve a man with a lifetimes experience these boats were a breathtaking sight; gleaming hulls, tall spars, and flags of five nations.

'How did they get *Avocet* here from Plymouth with no mainsail?' asked Johnny.

'I wish you wouldn't put a wet blanket on a lovely day,' Steve grumbled. The whole incident still rankled.

'At least we're in the clear,' said Kirsten. 'I've had an email from Shilltinberg's office in Zurich and they've as good as said they'll order a new one from us.'

'Shilltinberg's backing the Banner in this libel suit. I guess he doesn't like Mr Crickerman.'


On the following Monday the police held their long promised press conference. Dave arrived early at constabulary HQ and found a seat near the front of the room. On each chair were sheets of A4 paper. Dave could see that these were photographs of a sort. They were the computer enhanced versions of the CCTV pictures from Hamble. Dave looked at each in turn. The man in the shots was definitely Alfred Ollavasen and the slight figure now much better defined was probably Michelle but he wasn't sure. Dave had only seen the woman once and briefly in Olifa in a bar. Other people would have to confirm her identity for certain and that included poor Emily and Tom.

The room was crowded now with crime reporters from all the national papers as well as two television crews. The police entered and took their places at the long rectangular table. They were led by Chief Superintendent Hollins, but the meeting was conducted by DCI Marchway.

'Ladies and gentlemen, thank you for your interest and support,' Marchway began. Could Dave detect a trace of irony? 'We think it is time to update you on the murder of Alfred Ollavasen. This man was brutally murdered by an assailant who stabbed him in the area of the throat three times. We assess this to have been a premeditated crime although any motive at the moment is unclear. The enhanced CCTV images that you have were all taken some weeks before the murder. We cannot prove a connection but we would very much appreciate if the female in the photos would come forward and talk to us.'

Hollins took over. 'You may ask questions.'

This was Dave's moment. 'There are several people myself included who can give you a very likely name for the woman in the pictures. Will you be giving out this name?'

'I'm sorry, Mr Manning, but we cannot do that. Not on the strength of very poor images. Such a thing is outside our remit.'

'BBC,' said a little man in a blue suit. 'Have you found the murder weapon?'

'Our forensic officers estimate the weapon to be a pointed double-sided knife of at least six inches in length. We have searched the site including using divers in the water but so far no trace. Our forensic officers have also made an inch-by-inch search of the land for evidence and anything that might give us a DNA profile. I cannot at this stage give you these results.'

Another journalist took up Dave's point. 'We've already heard that the woman in the pictures has been named. Will you be trying to trace this person by her name?'

Marchway replied smoothly. 'We are pursuing every avenue and we are confident of a resolution.'

Typical cop speak thought Dave and we're all none the wiser. Well, there was nothing to stop him looking for Michelle Le Bois himself. She couldn't scare him and he was curious as to why she would kill Ollavasen. Maybe she was a psycho by nature or more likely the man tried to molest her.

Chief Superintendent Hollins doubted if this press conference had taken the heat off his investigation. The rapacious pack was not satisfied; the police had told them nothing because frankly there was nothing to tell and the press corps knew it. Of course the police nationally would be searching for the last whereabouts of this Le Bois woman. They had already checked her and she had form: six months jail in France for vandalism and expelled from Olifa during the last Olympics. He would have to ask the Olifarian police for the details. As he walked to the car he was intercepted by Garry Marchway with a paper in his hand. As he came closer Hollins could see it was an email printout.

'Here's a surprise,' said Garry. 'We've traced Crickerman's helicopter and it landed on our patch at Streatway airfield and where's that?'

'Garry don't keep us in suspense. I've heard of it but that's all. You tell me.'

'It's a gliding club a mile away from Greatswood Manor and that is the UK home of Erich Shilltinberg.'

'I thought those two were on bad terms. Shilltinberg is giving Hengist Crickerman a hard time with this libel business.'

'The point is,' said Hollins. 'It seems that Crickerman was in

Hampshire at the time of the murder, but just a twenty minute drive from the Hamble. Does this really have any relevance for us?'

'I dunno', said Marchway. 'But why didn't he admit where he was going to you straight up instead of that rubbish about a night with the office girl?'

'Garry, we're in very murky waters. Were you around at the time of the Lindgrune case?'

'I was walking the beat in Wimbledon but we heard rumours.'

'I was here in Hampshire. We had a senior superintendent in Portsmouth called Frank Matheson. Frank was close to rumbling Lindgrune and then there came an order from the Home Office to back off. Matheson refused and it cost him his career.'

Garry looked worried. 'Can they do that?'

'Where money and politics is concerned you bet they can and will. So we must be circumspect and keep the names of these boys to ourselves.'

Dave Manning had spent the morning on the telephone to Copenhagen. It had taken him the best part of an hour to track down Peter Jurgen but in this case the Banner would pick up the tab for the phone bill. Peter was a leading Danish yachting correspondent who Dave had bumped into at various sailing venues around the globe. Better than that, Peter had been a crewman on the Scandinavian challenge in the same world circling yacht race that Dave had sailed in for New Zealand.

'Hi there old comrade,' Peter's singsong accent echoed down the line. 'How you doing?'

'Doing fine, thanks. Got a steady job with a tabloid and it gets better. I'm marrying my girl at Christmas.'

'Hey, man, Christmas. Bit cold then won't it?'

Dave laughed. 'Not in Auckland New Zealand. Christmas is midsummer then.'

'Ah, and congratulations. Pretty girl is she?'

'Too right, mate. She's called Josie and I love her.'

'That is very good. So, how can I help you?'

'You've heard about the Ollavasen murder?'

'You bet damn well we have. Our tabloids have gone bonkers.'

Good, thought Dave. Now I may get somewhere. 'Peter, what do you know about the girl that Ollavasen assaulted?'

'Oh yes, that got the man in the deepest shit. He was lucky to miss jail. But I think the girl was not Danish. I cannot remember her name but I am sure she was English.'

'Dave was surprised. 'But I thought this incident was in Denmark.'

'Oh yes, it was near the yacht club in Hellerup. Bad business and I tell you, Dave. We think he should not be murdered, but same time that man's no loss.'

'Peter, if the girl was English I would like to talk to her. If you can find out her name I'd be grateful.'

'Wait patient, old friend. I am not in my office but I have my lap top. There we have lots of info.'

Dave sat patiently with the phone set clapped to his ear.

'Here we go,' said Peter. 'Sammy, or Samantha Halderholm, from Bath in England.' Peter cackled with laughter. 'That's a big joke. You Aussies say English never take a bath.'

'Correction old mate. I am not a bloody Aussie. Look, can you tell me anything about this girl. Was she a looker, what made Ollavasen go apeshit?'

'I think I understand that you mean. Was she beautiful? My friend, indeed she was and she was fortunate that night. Her brother saw what happened and he saved her and then he called the police.'

'From what I gather Ollavasen got what was coming to him after that. What about this Samantha's brother. What can you tell me about him?'

'Oh, big strong guy by all accounts but not big enough to lay flat Ollavasen. He tried the retribution on his own before the police come, but Ollavasen half killed him, so this Mr Halderholm bears a double grudge.'

'Yeah, Peter, I guess he does just that.' Dave muttered his thanks and rang off. He had learned things that could put him and the Daily Banner one jump ahead of the bumbling Hampshire police

Tom really felt for his wife, but what could he do? Her ebullience and usual chatter had vanished overnight and now she was depressed and nervous. Emily and little Peter were the most precious things in his world. He could never forgive the Le Bois girl. Tom had been within seconds of death from the gun of a madman and it was Michelle Le Bois who had screamed at the guy urging him to shoot. Emily knew that of course and the same delusional man had tried to have Emily's baby aborted. Since their return from South America and their wedding they had forgotten all about Michelle Le Bois and neither knew nor cared where she was. Now the woman was out there somewhere, maybe watching them and it seemed she might be a ruthless killer.

Tom went to find Emily. She was in their room lying on the bed with Peter curled up beside her. She gave him a wan smile. 'Tom, darling, Tony Travis rang when you were out. He wants me to go to London for a briefing on this libel case.'

'What did you say?'

'I told him what's happened and I said I can't leave Peter.' Now she was sobbing. 'Oh Tom, what if she's out here now just waiting to snatch our baby.'

'You can take Peter with you; he's a good boy and much quieter now.'

Emily shook her head. 'I wouldn't feel safe anywhere.'

'Then I've got another suggestion. I happen to know that your friend Chloe has ten days leave. Her whole unit has it before overseas deployment. Dave Manning rang me and suggested that if you were really uptight about Le Bois, Chloe would stay here with a couple of nasty tough squaddies.'

'You must stay too.'

'Just while you're away. Take your mobile and ring in as often as you like.'

Emily thought for a while and then looked up and smiled. 'Ok, but you feed Peter. You and Lily Lorrimer. Don't let Chloe near him.'

Tom laughed. 'Too right I won't. She's three parts a man anyway. What does she know?'


Dave rang the editor of the Banner and asked if the paper could track the whereabouts of this Samantha Halderholm. He then emailed his account of that morning's press conference. Unsatisfactory would hardly describe it. Dave still did not buy the idea that the murder was connected with the libel case or even with Ollavasen trying to throw a yacht race. A sexual motive was far more likely and some women folk including his Josie would probably say Alfred had it coming. He decided to go and have a look at the competing super-yachts now docked at Gunwharf quay at the entrance to Portsmouth Harbour. This was just a short drive down the M27 and through Portsmouth. He smiled when he thought about these strange British traditions. Southampton where he had been was only twenty plus miles from Portsmouth but these were two cities that might as well be a thousand mile apart. Rivalry based around football could almost be described as sectarian. It was intense and this rivalry sometimes seeped into other areas. He guessed Southampton yachtsmen would not be pleased to hear that these maxi yachts had chosen Portsmouth for their public display.

Dave didn't think much of football or soccer as he knew it. As a New Zealander it was rugby that was the game that inspired and excited him. The Brits could keep their round ball rubbish.

The big yachts were certainly awesome. He walked along the dockside staring rubbernecked in company with a sizeable crowd of spectators. It was yet another hot day and the quay was bright with the wearers of style jeans and bright summer dresses. He had hoped to see the *Qualistores* crewman called Ed, but in that he was disappointed or at least he was until he saw the group assembling on that yacht's deck. A photographer was posing a group of girls attired in the skimpiest bikinis. Dave couldn't help himself; he had to stop along with a sizeable crowd to take in this delightful scene. Then he had a fresh surprise. One of the girls he knew. She was pretty, shapely, blonde and tanned. There was no doubt she was Susanna, Chloe's girl. He shrugged and continued ogling. Well why shouldn't Susanna enjoy the sun and wear a bikini? She might be gay, a pity that – but so what.

An hour later he headed for home in Bayswater. He arrived at the flats, parked the car and called out as he entered the entrance hall. Josie smiled at him as she looked up from her computer. 'How's the new book?' he asked.

She frowned. 'I've had one good idea and I think the first two chapters will do but now I'm stuck.'

He walked across and gently lifted her from the chair. 'Come on upstairs. Let's get naked.'

She giggled and threw her arms around him. 'Hey, whatever's brought this on?'

Emily was feeling a little better. Nothing had happened in the last forty eight hours and Chloe and her bodyguard were due to arrive tomorrow. She was even looking forward to her trip to the Travis chambers. Immersion in this libel case might distract from her worries. Little Peter was settling down well to feeding and sleeping.

All the tales of screaming mayhem that she had been fed before birth had proved untrue. Maybe she would pay for it with the next birth. Would there be a next time? She would like it but in the long run it was down to Tom. She had enough of breast feeding and Peter was taking some sustenance from a bottle. As for Tom; his long period of celibacy was beginning to get to him. Eventually she would need to relent although right now she had no appetite for bedroom romps.

She started in alarm as she heard the key in the front door. No, don't be so stupid, it was only Lily Lorrimer come to take her turn as nanny. Lily was a stout dark-haired village girl who had had three infants herself. Nothing whatever fazed Lily and Emily was eternally grateful for her help and support. Today Lily seemed excited about something.

Emily smiled at her. 'What's the problem?'

'I think I've seen that woman as the police are looking for.'

Emily felt cold. 'What woman.'

'The one in those pictures that's been on telly.'

'Are you really sure?'

'I told you I do cleaning on Wednesdays over at Greatswood in that big house.'

'I know it. I've seen it in the distance but I've never been in there.'

'Belongs to a foreign gentleman, but he's not always there. Anyway on Wednesday I was cleaning the landing upstairs where the bedrooms are and one of the doors opened and this woman was standing there. Then she saw me and shot back in the room like a scared rabbit and slammed the door.'

'Lily, you will have to tell the police.'

Lily looked rueful. 'I can't be certain it's the one in those pictures but she looked like it. But if she's a guest and nothing to do with the murder I could lose that job and the foreign man pays good money.'

Emily didn't know what to think. Could it really be Michelle Le Bois in hiding and not ten miles away? Her personal nightmare was beginning to come true. It could all be Lily's imagination but why should this mysterious guest hide away like that?

'Please, Lily. You must tell the police.'

'Yeah, all right.'

Emily went downstairs and rang the police herself. She was passed to a girl in the incident room and then to a Chief Inspector Marchway. Mention of Greatswood Manor was clearly unwelcome. 'Thank you, Mrs Stoneman but I must ask your witness to call in and talk to us. That would be most helpful'

Emily put the phone back and sighed. Mention of Greatswood had been a clear turn off for this senior copper. But she resolved to drive Lily, plus Peter to the Hamble incident room now this moment. But before that she rang Dave Manning on his mobile and told him what she'd heard.

Dave took Emily's call while he was covering the opening of a new chandlery business in Waterlooville. He quickly slipped away and took the road for Greatswood. He found the place on his road map and entered it into the satnav. Greatswood was a tiny Hamlet of few dwellings and one vast Georgian pile of a stately home. All his newshound senses were buzzing. If it was true that Shilltinberg's UK house was the hiding place of a murder suspect then that was sensation enough. That apart, nothing in this scenario made a grain of sense. Even if Shilltinberg had wanted Ollavasen removed, Michelle Le Bois was a very unlikely choice as hitman.

Dave left the M27 and began to drive north through the Meon valley. A grubby road  sign and the satnav told him to turn left for Greatswood. He was now in a very narrow lane with high banks to either side and inevitably he came head to head with one gigantic green tractor. This one was towing a high grain trailer and was not inclined to reverse. Born into a farm community himself, Dave could relate to this. Gingerly he reversed twenty yards and pulled into a gateway. He drove onward again and then without warning the lane opened to reveal a mown village green with five whitewashed cottages, a pub and a tiny church. On the opposite side to the cottages he could see a lodge and a pair of fine gates. The irritating voice on the satnav told him he had *"arrived at your destination"*.

Now what? He had arrived, what should be his next move? Dave's old mentor, tabloid veteran Sid Everett would have marched straight up to the house and battered on the front door. He would then have bluffed his way past the butler with some phoney story and found his way indoors. Even if he was subsequently thrown off the premises Sid would have thought that par for the course. Although Dave was a Kiwi from downunder he did not have Sid's brass-necked cheek, nor his immunity to verbal abuse. He would have to be a bit more subtle. He left the car and gazed around. This really was a delightful spot and so very English. He walked across to the high gates and noted the CCTV camera mounted on one of the supporting stone posts.

He went back to the car and had another look at the map; hopeless far too small scale. He noticed for the first time a smart new wooden sign for a footpath. The direction was pointing to the big house just visible through the trees. The ground was dry and sympathetic to his smart town shoes. Yes, and binoculars could come in handy. He reached in the car for them. The path ran parallel to the entrance drive and began to climb along a grassy bank. The great house was in view now and it was impressive. Dave panned around the binoculars but he could see no human figure. He walked on. Although it was hot the path was pleasantly shaded with ash and beech trees. Looking down he could see a tennis court and a large covered swimming pool. There was opulence here no doubt of that. He was much closer to the house now and he could see a terrace with little garden tables and chairs. A man was sitting at one of the tables reading a newspaper a glass of red wine and a bottle in front of him. I bet he's not reading the Banner, Dave smiled to himself. He focused the binoculars and now he had a real shock, a shock that almost made him drop the glasses. The man had half turned and Dave knew him and the sight brought back bad memories. What in hell's name was this character doing sitting there sunning himself in rural Hampshire. Dave resumed his watch as he saw the man rise from his seat and walk into the house through the wide veranda glass doors. His mobile phone was ringing. Dave groped inside his jacket for it. 'Hi there, Janet, what news?'

Janet was the Banner editor's secretary. 'Hi Dave, we've found your Samantha Halderholm.'

'That's great quick work.'

'Yes, but she no longer lives in Bath. She's in your territory working in the yacht business. Let me see…' there was a pause. 'Yes, that's it she works in the office of Mulberry Lane Yacht Charters in Hamble River.'

Emily drove her Nissan with Lily sitting in the back seat with Peter in his safety seat. The little boy had been fractious but the car journey seemed to soothe him. They arrived at Hamble Point to find that the police tapes had gone and the marina was getting back to something like normal working. They reached the incident room but of course Inspector Marchway had already left. A woman sergeant took Lily's statement.

'Will you follow this up?' Emily asked.

'We follow up everything and all evidence until we reach a resolution and make an arrest.'

Emily felt too tired to try and argue. She knew from personal experience in court that the police were wary of influential rich names. She and Lily had done their duty. Now home and report to Tom.

# CHAPTER 12

Chloe arrived noisily. As Tom remarked she could hardly arrive in any other way. In fact it was something of an army convoy that pulled up outside the Bishops Sutton home of Emily and Tom. Chloe and Susanna appeared in a large four by four Honda with a stack of tents aboard. Two other cars appeared shortly afterwards and disembarked four ominous looking soldiers in civilian jeans and T-shirts.

'We can stay here for a week,' said Chloe. 'After that let's hope the cops have caught that Michelle. Anyway she won't want to tangle with me again, not after what we did to her in France that time.'

Emily remembered all too well that night in Hyres when they caught this same Michelle sabotaging their boat.

'This is Corporal Mike,' Chloe pointed at a large man with tattooed arms. 'And these are Privates: Ian, Matt and Ross, but we're not standing on rank here any of us. So first names only eh?'

Emily sat everyone down in the kitchen and Tom briefed them on the latest news about Michelle and Lily Lorrimer's testimony.

'How far away is this Greatswood House,' asked Chloe.

'About ten miles from here – near West Meon.'

Certainly the four soldiers were a formidable bunch and Emily was relieved to see them. She was still confused about Lily's evidence. She might have dismissed it but for the part where the alleged Michelle had bolted at the sight of a stranger in the house. Whatever happened she couldn't see Michelle wanting a second encounter with Chloe let alone the four toughs she had brought with her. On the other hand let her come and then they could hand her to the police.

Emily could only hope the police would at least visit the Greatswood house. She was worried and feeling a bit guilty.

'Chloe, shouldn't these soldiers be with their own families?'

'No,' said Chloe. 'All these have volunteered. They're single men – like the idea of a new adventure.'

Emily's unspoken question was how come these sexy hunks were single? But that would be bad taste.

The police car arrived at Greatswood House at nine o'clock in the morning.

'This is something else,' remarked the first constable. 'Not the sort of place we usually find a villain.'

'Oh well, let's go see,' said his companion.

They marched to the front door and rang the bell. It was answered after a long interval by a butler. There was no doubt who this character was; he even wore a tail coat.

'Gentlemen, how can I assist you?' The voice was a bit of a let down. Not posh, but refined Dorset.

'We have information that you have a guest here who we would like to speak to.'

'Herr Shiltinberg is not at home but we do have a lady and a gentleman staying with us.'

The constable had a feeling he was an actor in some TV period drama. He played his card and showed the man the photo fit picture.

'I don't think I can help you there,' the man replied. 'We have a Mrs Wenman staying here. Would you care to speak to her?'

'Yes, please.'

'Gentlemen, please this way.'

The pair followed the butler into the house. It was less lavish than they had expected although some of the paintings on the walls looked like genuine old masters.

'We can advise you on security,' said the first constable.

'Thank you sir, but we have that angle well covered.'

The second constable wondered how this decorous, heavily dressed and almost robotic figure kept cool on a day as hot as this. The Butler led them through a pair of high French windows and out onto a terrace with little tables and garden chairs. A man and a woman were sitting there and the sight was an immediate disappointment. The woman was fair-haired, middle-aged and heavily built while the man had swarthy features although definitely not Asian.

'Mrs Wenman,' said the butler. 'These gentlemen would like a word with you.'

'Jeez, what am I supposed to have done?' she smiled. The voice was American or Canadian the constable wasn't sure which.

'As I am aware, madam you haven't done anything that would concern us. We are asking if this woman in the picture has been here at any time recently.'

The woman took the picture and stared at it. 'Don't know her.'

'Thank you. That's all we wanted to ask.'

The butler showed them out and they walked to the car. 'Know what I think?' said the first constable.

'The old biddy was nervous when you showed her that photo fit.'

'You bet she was and she was lying through her teeth as was that poncy butler.'

Lily was looking after Peter for the day so Emily could take the train for Waterloo from Alton Station. Chloe was relaxing in the garden. Tom had briefed the army guys about Michelle Le Bois and right then they were making an inspection of the nearby woods and then the village itself.

Susanna had taken the Honda and gone shopping. As Chloe put it they had five very hungry extra mouths to feed. Tom had resumed work and was due to upgrade a computer system in Yeovil.

For Chloe all was peaceful. From where she sat she could see fields and cows. A tractor was turning hay nearby and she could catch the scent. It was almost like home. Then Lily appeared carrying the portable phone. It was Dave Manning and could he speak to Emily? Chloe explained that Emily was in London in conference with Tony Travis. It was nice, thought Chloe to hear a Kiwi accent even if the speaker was a journo.

'I can give you Em's mobile number if that'll help,' she said.

'No, I don't want to upset her on a day when she's back to work but I can tell you, Chlo. You'll never guess who I saw earlier. The bastard was sitting sunning himself outside a swank house drinking wine.'

'Dave, you silly sod. Will you please explain?'

He told her and Chloe felt a rush of pure anger. 'Dave, are you sure?'

'Too right I am.'

'What in hell is that guy doing around here? Look I'm not going to tell Em yet. She's got enough worries. You never saw that Michelle?'

'Not a sign when I was there.'

'If it's the same guy, well good! Then I can give him a piece of my mind. I'll enjoy that.'


Michelle Le Bois watched the two policemen leave. That was it, time for her to get out.
If the law was this close then it was time to move. She had money on her and her car was parked outside that pub. She was grateful to Wendy for giving her refuge, but she was in a dodgy situation. Could she talk her way out of this? It was the question she'd asked a hundred times. She didn't trust the police. Would they bother with her evidence when it would be so easy to fit her up with the crime and put

her away for life? She hadn't committed any murder but she'd been there and as good as seen it happen. Her appointment with Ollavasen had been set for ten o'clock that evening. She had the information and the passwords ready to hand to the brute. This time she wouldn't get too close. She wasn't giving that lecherous gorilla another chance to molest her. She had reached the marina and was on her way to the rendezvous when the lights went out. There was no moon and for a moment she felt blind until her night vision kicked in. Then she heard it; an awful gurgling scream, followed by a splash. Michelle hadn't waited; she turned and fled.

She had her bag packed already. The South American man was out on the terrace with that Wendy. She could see the snooty butler serving the Dago more wine. The coast was clear. She tiptoed, barefoot, down the wide staircase carrying her shoes.  Outside she replaced the shoes, skirted the tennis courts and made it to the wide footpath for the village. She must reach her car and then what? Get out of this country. She had the passwords for half a million dollars salted away in a tax haven. How could she get there when every airport and port was watching for her. A new identity was the answer and she could afford to pay for it. She stiffened with alarm. Someone was on the path following her and catching up fast.

She spun round and then relaxed. 'Oh no, not you again – how did you get here?'

The knife split her throat and neck.

## CHAPTER 13

When Inspector Marchway arrived in Greatswood the scene of crime was already secured and a forensic team was scouring the ground. 'How is our witness?' he asked.

'He's pretty shook up, sir,' the constable told him. 'The man was walking his dog and came across the body. The assailant must've run off before he could conceal it. Could have seen our witness coming and done a runner. He's lucky he could've got it too.'

'Where is the witness now?'

'In the pub sir and we've a WPC with him.'

Marchway found the witness in the snug bar that had temporarily been sealed off from the outside world. He was a stocky, fortyish man dressed for walking including stout boots. Mercifully someone had bought him a pint of beer that he was sipping nervously. His Labrador dog lay beside him apparently asleep and oblivious.

'Thank you, sir for your help. I'm Detective Chief Inspector Marchway from Southampton CID. Can I have your name, sir.'

'Philip Evans.' The man had a soft London accent. 'Please Inspector. Is the woman the one in your photos?'

'We have no formal identification yet and we can't be involved in guessing.'

'You see the poor girl was lying on her back when we came up to her. She was covered in blood but I think I could give you a name – Michelle Le Bois.'

Marchway was alert. Was he dealing with a suspect? It was all possible although Mr Evans did not look like a murderer. But then who could tell?

'Mr Evans, please could you give me an account of your movements this day?'

'Yes, I can do that and please. I didn't kill her but I knew her.'

'In what context?'

'She is or was a journalist of a sort; did freelance for several sheets but she also hung around the sailing scene. Don't think she sailed herself but she seemed to have some sort of vendetta against those little girls that won gold in Olifa last year.'

'Do you know why?'

'No, and it didn't make her popular. Everyone loves them.'

'Unusual name. Was she French?'

'Didn't seem so. Spoke English as good as any of us.'

Marchway stood up. He smiled supportively. Somehow he didn't see this man as a murderer. 'Thank you, Mr Evans for your help. An officer will take a statement as to your movements and then you can go home. But you must be available should we wish to talk to you again.'

'My car's parked at West Meon and I can't walk back you've closed the footpath.'

'Don't worry, sir. We'll give you a ride there in a police car. Just let the officer know when you feel ready.'

Now Marchway had a dilemma. The dead woman was within a stone's throw of the house where a witness had reported seeing someone amazingly similar. His officers had already called at the house and the inhabitants had denied any such person was there. He didn't have enough evidence to go on, or nothing like enough for him to search that house and grill the occupants. He sighed, he was a policeman with ambition and an eye on his career and crossing a man as wealthy and influential as this Shilltinberg was a risk he'd rather not take. He went out into the sunlight had a word with the forensic team and then drove back to his office. He had a feeling, an intuition almost, that it was time he found out more about Alfred Ollavasen and this long distance yacht race.

Emily found she had stepped back in time. Life in the legal chambers was unchanged from her days as a pupil. The staff, the routine, the other lawyers were all there with the same in-house gossip. Emily was a little embarrassed when Tony Travis introduced her to his two current pupils and somehow held her up to be a shining example. The libel defence had stalled somewhat. The murder of Ollavasen had been a setback. Tony had been certain that the man would have turned and been persuaded to confess his part in the scam. Now it seemed that the prosecution was targeting Easterbroke Sails once more. That, thought Emily was not going to improve her grumpy old Dad's temper.

She was able to report a little about events at Hamble and fill in technical details about the maxi yachts. She concealed her own fears; they didn't seem relevant here and she didn't want to play the hysterical female in a place where she was respected. But it was a nostalgic visit meeting old friends even if not much was gained with the libel case. Following a good lunch, Tony found her a taxi and she rode back to the station to join her train for Alton.

She reached Bishops Sutton in time for a cup of tea and the six o'clock news on television. No longer was there talk of the Hamble murder on the local news, thank God. It seemed even here in the countryside they lived in an increasingly violent world. A fresh murder of an unidentified woman had happened on a footpath near West Meon. The police were being especially tight lipped for some reason. If there was another madman on the loose then they were fairly safe with Chloe and her four guys on patrol.

She comforted herself with a happy half hour with Peter who was beginning to utter a word she couldn't comprehend. Suddenly she was feeling better, she couldn't think why but that night she finally relented and let her husband have sex. What started as a wifely duty soon turned into an hour of delight for both of them.

Dave Manning found the offices of Mulberry Lane Yacht Charters up the side lane of that name in Hamble. He parked the Renault beside a black Volvo with a small dent in the passenger side door. He walked over and stared inside. Somewhere he'd seen this car with its minor damage before. The interior was empty but apparently well spruced and cared for. The office was a wholly unpretentious place; in fact a wooden prefabricated building with a bow window filled with lavish photographs of sailing yachts. Nice ones too, he mused but mostly too big for he and Josie to handle on their own. Well, he wasn't going to reveal his true identity. On this occasion he was definitely a potential customer. He opened the door and walked inside.

The interior was dark after the bright sunlight outside and it took a few seconds for his eyes to refocus. The room was well furnished with a wooden desk two computer screens on the desk and a comfortable leather sofa for visitors. That apart there was no sign of life except for the soft playing of piped music from somewhere. Dave looked around for a bell to ring or a buzzer to press but found neither. Then the door behind the desk opened and a voice called. 'Can you wait a moment, please and someone will be with you.'

'That's fine.' Dave called back. 'No problem.'

A few minutes later a man entered, presumably the manager. He was an impressive figure clad in jeans and a sports shirt and definitely a genuine yachtsman. His tanned features and general demeanour was the real thing. 'How can I help you,' the voice was genial, but had that smooth English public school timbre that always irritated Dave.

'I'm interested in a holiday charter. Do you have anything easy to handle and based in the Med?'

'Indeed we have six there, but I must warn you we will insist on you taking one of our approved skippers. Tell me do you have experience?'

Dave was irritated by the patronising tone, but he wasn't going to admit to anything that would give away his identity, or not yet. 'I've done a bit of sailing.'

'Ah, in Australia?'

This man was making a dangerous mistake; telling a Kiwi he was an Aussie always riled. 'That's right,' Dave replied.

For ten minutes the manager pulled up yacht details on his computer. Dave had a good look at the man. He was the sort of smooth character who would have no trouble pulling the girls or in his case the more mature ladies. Classically handsome some would say with his slicked black hair and rugged jaw. Dave was drawn into the part he had to play and was soon thinking a Mediterranean cruise might be a real tonic for he and Josie, or at least until the man began to lay out the fees and costs.

Dave thanked the man and took a handful of brochures. 'Tell me,' he asked. 'My fiancée met a lady called Samantha Halderholm and I rather gathers she works for you.'

'Oh yes,' the man grinned. 'I'm Richard Halderholm and Sammy's my sister, but she away from work for a few days. Can I give her your name or rather your fiancée's?'

'Yes, Josephine Pallent, but we all call her Josie.'

'I will let you into a secret,' said Richard Halderholm. 'Samantha has had a difficult year. She ran our office in Copenhagen; we do a lot of Baltic charters these days. Then one of our skippers assaulted her; well frankly he tried to rape the girl and it's left her in a shocked state.'

Dave nodded. 'I seem to have read about this somewhere.'

'Probably, but I'll tell your more. The bastard was Ollavasen the man that was knifed last week and good job too.' The tone had changed as the man's eyes gleamed with unrestrained hate.

Yes, thought Dave. By all accounts you took him on and got pulped. So you had a score to settle apart from your poor sister.

'So, you won't be at his funeral,' said Dave.

'No, but I'll go to spit on his grave.'

Dave left the Mulberry office and walked back to his car. This Richard Halderholm worried him. He seemed a pleasant enough guy on first appearances but there was just something about the man, a tension below the surface that Dave suspected could trigger into rage or worse. Where had he seen that black Volvo? If he owned a plush car like that he would have hammered out the dent in the passenger side door. He turned and walked back to his own motor. Then the memory returned – Plymouth; that was it.

Dave drove the short distance from Hamble and into the city of Southampton. Once again he had a favour to call in from the local paper. Rob who covered sailing was in; Dave had checked before on his mobile.

'Hi, Dave,' Rob grinned a greeting. 'How can we help the scurrilous Banner?'

'Hey, that's pots and kettles,' Dave laughed. 'Look, this is in confidence but I would like to know a bit about Richard Halderholm from Mulberry Yacht Charters. Is it true he had a run in with the police?'

Rob looked surprised. 'Well, he did as a matter of fact, but he had some cause and the charge was dropped.'

'Can you tell me what exactly happened?'

'Yes, Halderholm parked his car up a side road with parking spaces, but he was careless and he left one front wheel an inch or so over the line. So along comes a cowboy wheel clamper and says he's going to clamp him and Halderholm will have to pay four hundred nicker to get unlocked. So Halderholm swings a good left hook and cowboy hits the deck. Halderholm picks up the clamp and heaves it over a fence.'

'So, he got done for assault.'

'Yeah, but the police and the magistrates had had about enough of these cowboys so Halderholm got off with a warning.'

'Was that the end of it? I mean I've heard the guy has a pretty short fuse.'

'I don't know him that well. But I know he had it in for that bastard Ollavasen.'

'He had good reason. Ollavasen tried to rape his sister.'

'I know that: Samantha Halderholm. It was in Copenhagen: we had an agency report at the time. I tried to talk to her brother, but he got stroppy and threw me out.'

Dave did some quick thinking. 'Look, Rob, you follow the sailing scene around these parts?'

'Yeah, that's my job.'

'Good, now anything you hear about the Halderholms, or Ed Coulden let me know and if it's juicy I'll get you a sub from the

Banner.'

'You reckon one of them did it. I mean knife Ollavasen?'

'They had motive. One of them could've done it. I don't know, Rob. I also don't know how I got dragged into all this, but the police are dumb. They're getting nowhere.'

Dave was partly correct. Inspector Marchway now had two murders on his hands and both were enigmas. It was just inside possibility that the second dead person was the murderer of the first. He certainly had never experienced a case like that. If so then the murderer would never be seen in court. He had nothing that could be proved and as things stood he couldn't even get a positive identification of the second body: that of the woman at Greatswood. The witness Evans had given him a name and a certain amount of information had trickled in to the office during the day.

Michelle Le Bois was a loner who did work as a freelance journalist. It appeared that she had no living relatives and no partner. She had an aunt and a cousin in New Zealand but had probably never met them. He had only three persons who could identify the woman and he wasn't keen to ask any of them. One was Sid Everett the veteran tabloid crime hack. Second a former flatmate of Michelle's who had not seen her for three years and finally Emily Stoneman and her husband Tom. He really didn't want to involve those two as he had heard that both had been threatened by Michelle Le Bois; to do with a yacht race or was it something else.

He had a vague memory in which the name Le Bois kept echoing. It was to do with another violent death and he couldn't remember when or where. One hope left; Ollavasen had a potential DNA sample. In the grip of the dead man's right hand had been a tiny slither of skin and hair. They weren't Ollavasen's and could have come from anywhere but there must be a good chance they were the murderers. If there was a match with the Greatswood body then that would be a big step forward.

It might have been had he not begun to uncover an unsavoury side to Ollavasen. He had one conviction already for sexual assault. That had been in Denmark two years ago. It seemed that had had no calming effect on the man; no further brushes with the law, but several unconfirmed reports of the man's violent sexual predilections had emerged. It was more than possible that this crime might just be covered as self-defence. No not with a sharp knife. Knives like that were carried by gangs of youths. There was evidence that Ollavasen had a taste for violent sex, but no record of him assaulting teenage girls. Marchway sighed: time to report to his chief.

At Greatswood the forensic team had drawn a blank. The earth on the footpath was baked hard and not a footprint to be seen; either assailant or victim. The body had been removed to the mortuary lab and only the white tape outline remained. The uniform sergeant had walked back to the pub. The plain clothes officers had pushed off home, not that he had been too impressed with them. Wet behind the ears young upstarts was his opinion. The pub landlord was waiting for him.

'Terrible this for business,' the man grumbled.

'You may well be surprised,' said the sergeant.

'Tell you one thing,' said the landlord. 'Can you do anything to get this car shifted?' He pointed to a new style Mini parked under the trees at the far side of the car park. 'It's been there for over ten days and we don't know whose it is.'

'Well, I can find that out for you.' The sergeant noted the registration number and reached for his mobile phone. The information came as a shock. 'Christ, we'd better get that moved and isolated ASAP.' The owner was one, Ms M Le Bois.

# *CHAPTER 14*

Dave Manning received the phone call at seven o'clock on the morning following his visit to Greatswood. Josie was still asleep and Dave was not at his best as he rolled towards the bedside phone. He sat up when he found he was talking to the editor of the Banner.

'Dave, I want you to fly to Zurich today.'

'Eh?'

'Yep, all expenses paid airline ticket bought, nice hotel the other end.'

'All right, what am I supposed to be looking for?'

The editor replied. 'You are to seek an interview with Mr. Erich Shilltinberg at the head office of Avocet Computers. But you are doing that in your capacity as the Daily Banner's yachting correspondent.'

Dave was still baffled. 'I doubt he'll see me with no appointment.'

'Frankly, Dave, I don't think any appointment would work.'

'How so?'

'Because we've been checking all our sources for the last week and it is beginning to look as if no such person exists. The man was a famous sportsman in his youth. There's no doubt that he built a business but for the last few years there seems to be no trace of him,' the editor paused and Dave heard some rustling paper work. 'So, David, off you go to Zurich and find out everything you can about Avocet Computers. Talk to employees or go to bed with the likely female ones. Just learn all you can about Shilltinberg.'

'All right, I'll try, but not your last bed suggestion.'

'Good man, call in here before you go and I'll brief you with more detail. Then it's to Gatwick and board your flight at five this evening,'

'Here's the report on Philip Evans,' said Marchway. 'It's not really helping though. Seems everything he told us checks out. He parked his car at West Meon locked it, put his dog on the lead, picked up his rucksack and started down the Greatswood path.'

'Ramblers,' Hollins grunted. 'Vegetarians.'

'That sounds impartial, sir,' grinned Marchway.

'How did Evans recognize the victim? Who is he what does he do for a living?'

Marchway checked his notes. 'Magazine editor in Surrey, published novelist, and he's a yachtie: got a boat at Chichester. Le Bois wrote a piece for his mag. Something to do with a litter clean up on Leith Hill.'

'I think you should do a house to house in West Meon,' said Hollins. 'Someone else went down that footpath.'

'Yes, sir. Le Bois was walking towards the Greatswood village and forensic are certain she was attacked by someone coming from behind her. Our officers walked the whole length and it's private land with nine foot deer fencing and there's no sign that anyone climbed over the fence.'

Hollins sighed audibly. 'We're going round in circles.'

Marchway replied. 'I've an idea myself that might be relevant. I think this could be connected with Ollavasen's sex life. We know he's got a record of sexual violence. One conviction in Denmark and several others suspected. Tell you what, sir. I want to assemble the whole of *Avocet Computers* crew and see what they can tell us.'

Susanna had arrived back the previous mid-afternoon with enough food to sustain a regiment let alone five hearty soldiers. Tom gave her a hand to unload. Apparently their guards had basic tastes as he discovered as he carried in bulk packs of baked beans, pies, corned beef, frozen fish and oven chips.

'You took your time,' Emily greeted Susanna. 'What kept you?'

'Had to go all the way to Qualistores outside Petersfield.' said Susanna. 'Gotta' shop with them as we've got this voucher that Hengist gave me. All the crew got one.'

'Seems he likes you,' said Tom.

'Well I got his boat across the pond both ways without hitting anything. But yeah, he's a great guy we all liked him, great to be around, and I can tell you; Ollavasen was a shit bastard.'

The soldiers had erected three drab tents on the front lawn. Two for themselves and one for Chloe and Susanna. 'That's CO's privilege,' Chloe laughed.

The call late next day came as an unwelcome diversion. 'This is Southampton police. Would it be possible for Mr and Mrs Stoneman to attend our main station?'

Tom was not pleased. 'We've already helped you with your enquiries. What's it this time?'

'My apologies but it's a very delicate matter. But would you help in identifying a dead person. We've had one name given us but we think you may be able to give a positive ID.'

Tom groaned. 'Well who is this dead person?'

'I'm unable to speculate but we think you may be able to give us a definite name.'

Tom rang off and went to find Emily. She was feeding Peter with his bottle. He explained.

'Have you any idea who they're talking about?' she asked.

'Look, I don't think you need come. I did this once before in Olifa with that Hammersen – remember. I don't want you upsetting yourself.'

'Oh come on, Tom. Drop the macho male and fragile female crap. Dead men don't bite and this is experience that might help my law career.'

'Who's going to look after Peter?'

'Nobody, he's coming with us. Anyway he finds car journeys soothing and sleep making.'

'Oh, bloody hell, it is her,' Emily clung to Tom all restraint gone as the tears fell down her face.

Tom turned to the officers. 'Her name is Michelle Le Bois. I should know; she once tried to kill me.'

'Mrs Stoneman,' asked the policeman. 'Can you confirm that identity?'

'Yes, that's her,' she spoke quietly. 'She hated me and I never knew why.'

'Thank you both,' replied the policeman. 'I know it's been hard for you, but these things have to be done.'

'Please,' Tom asked. 'Was she the woman we heard about – the one killed near Greatswood?'

'Well, that's no secret, but yes this is the one.'

Inspector Marchway had not expected this new experience but he was never going to refuse the offer. He had wanted to interview the crew of *Avocet Computers* and they were not only cooperating, they had invited him to sail with them from Portsmouth to Hamble, *Avcocet's* home port. Marchway knew very little about sailing his sport was golf, but the weather was fine and not too much wind so he had happily agreed.

Moored with several others alongside Gunwharf Quay the yacht looked massive. He failed to guess how many millions the sponsor company must have poured into this project. The crewmen, they were all men, but not the posh public school types he had expected. They were muscular and athletic and clearly devoted to their ship. He was helped onboard and immediately the warps were cast off, the fenders brought in and they were away. A massive diesel engine was driving the yacht while the sails remained furled.

A man called Terry was steering and he explained. 'Wind's south west and in our face. Much quicker do the passage under power.'

'I see you have a new main sail. Is that the right term?' Marchway looked at the huge boom spar overhead.

'That's it, mainsail, all one word, but it's not new. It was a throw out from another boat and it's old style terylene. The one that bust was Kevlar.'

Marchway looked at the man. Terry was an easy laid-back sort of character with a slight north-country accent. 'As you know it is the death of Mr Ollavasen that we are investigating and it seems there is a connection with your main sail.'

'Oh Alfred, yes,' said Terry. 'Fine seaman, got to give him that but there was something funny about that sail failure.'

'Go on.'

'It was blowing force eight and above for most of the trip home. So, we had a reef down and sometimes two most of the time. That means a sail area reduction. Then the wind dropped with not far to go so we shook out both reefs and the sail fell apart. I don't think it was the maker's fault. Someone had removed half the stitching on the lower panel. Set full main and bingo – it rips apart.'

'You had no spare?'

'No, but we were leading and only had a few hundred miles to go. We pleaded with him to forget the main and set our biggest spinnaker. Wind was astern we wouldn't have lost the race if he'd agreed.'

'In that case couldn't you have overruled him?'

'Not if we wanted to crew again. Mutiny on the *Bounty*- no way; and you didn't argue with Alfred not if you wanted to avoid a bloody nose.'

'What was your real opinion of Mr Ollavasen?'

'As I said fine seaman, but uncouth rough-neck bastard ashore. If you ask me he was a sort of Viking throwback.'

'Were you aware that he had a criminal conviction in Denmark?'

'No.'

'It was for serious sexual assault. He was given a suspended prison sentence and fined a sum of money that virtually bankrupted him.'

'My God, yes I can believe that. We caught him at it in Plymouth days before the big race started. He had this little girl in the yard behind a pub. Luckily three of our lads saw it and pulled him away. Alfred got really aerated told us the girl was gagging for it.'

'Was a complaint made to the police? I can check with my colleagues in Devon.'

'If she did complain you blokes never did anything and she wasn't the only one. You know the one you're talking about in Denmark. I think that could have been Ed Coulden's girl.'

'Who is he and what is the girl's name?'

'I don't know 'em that well, but Ed Coulden was in *Qualistores* crew with Crickerman and his girl was called…' Terry paused. 'I'm trying to think…Yeah, she's Sammy – that's her name. Works for Mulberry's office in Hamble.'

'Where can I find your Mr Coulden?'

'Right now he's probably at sea. He skippers part time for Mulberry the holiday charter setup.'

'So he and his lady would have a grievance against Mr Ollavasen.'

Terry laughed. 'Well, he can't bother the girls any more, not where he's gone. You say he'd been in trouble with the law in his own country.'

They had now come to the crux. 'Mr Ollavasen was in serious financial trouble,' said Marchway. 'Do you think he deliberately threw that race for cash? Think about it before you answer.'

Terry stood up and made a helm adjustment. 'Another mile and we turn for Hamble. But yes, on the face of it what happened looks pretty damning, but who would stick a knife in the sod just for that? I think it was a woman more like. Was it the one in your pictures?'

Marchway, was not to be drawn on Michelle Le Bois. 'No, that woman has been eliminated from our enquiries.'

Now for his last question. 'What can you tell me about this yacht's owner: Mr Erich Shilltinberg?'

'Not a lot – nothing really. The man's never come near us.' Terry stood up and called to his crew. 'Shake it, lads. Twenty minutes to dockside. Get those lines ready.'

Dave Manning had finally reached Zurich airport. The Banner had granted him most generous expenses so he was able to book a taxi for the ride south into town. The Banner had booked him into the Hotel St Gothard in Bahnhof Strasse. This had been chosen as it was only three blocks away from Avocet Computers head office. It was a comfortable hostelry family run and traditional. Dave unpacked and settled down in his room to wait the call for dinner. He now had time to work out his tactics for tomorrow.
It did occur to him that the Banner had invested quite a sum in cash for his trip and in return he should expect to give them something good.

The next morning Dave awoke early and walked down to the lakeside. In front of him stretched that beautiful sheet of water the Zurich See. Some small yachts were already sailing and trying to make headway against a shifting breeze. Dave had the impression of a gigantic version of Branham Lake in England where Steve Simpson raced his Paralympic keelboat. Otherwise the sight of this water made him a little bit homesick. He could have been on a stretch of coast in the South Island. He returned to the hotel and ate what passed for breakfast; now to business.

This city, one of the world's financial capitals was already busy. Expensive BMWs and Mercedes, even a solitary Rolls cruised the amazingly clean and trim streets. Everywhere smart suited pedestrians strode carrying fat briefcases. He stood in front of a fairly modest office block with the Avocet Computers Logo. It was old fashioned probably twenties or thirties build and one even entered the vestibule through revolving doors.

A formidable woman receptionist sat at an oval desk of polished wood and glass top. In front of her was a computer screen. Dave presented his card and a letter of introduction from the editor of the Banner. He wasn't sure how much these Swiss knew about the British tabloid press or what the reaction might be.

The woman actually managed a smile and then spoke in perfect English. 'I do not know if Herr Shilltinberg will see you. He you must understand is elderly now and he has not been well. But if your interest is only yachting then I will see what we can do.'

'Herr Shilltinberg is a yachtsman?' Dave asked. 'I know he has a very fine yacht in England.'

'Indeed had he not been stricken with illness as a young man he would have sailed for Helvetia in the 1948 Olympic Sailing.'

Dave made a quick calculation. That regatta had been staged nearly seventy years ago which would put this mysterious entrepreneur in his late eighties at least.

'I assume,' the receptionist continued, 'that you have a mobile phone that operates reliably in this city.'

'Of course.'

'Very well, Mr Manning give me the number and I will see what I can do.'

So that was it and Dave found himself out on the Strasse again. But he had achieved more than he expected. So Shilltinberg existed and was a genuine racing yachtsman. His health was poor which explained his reclusiveness. All he could do now was keep fingers crossed and hope for that exclusive interview.

Dave was drawn back to the lake. A small boat race was in progress with a turning mark near the shore where he stood. Tourist boats were leaving the dockside including a magnificent antique paddle steamer. It was such a peaceful happy scene. He wished Josie was with him; one day perhaps when they were married and had kids they would come back to this place to see this magnificent lake from the water. He was puzzled by the sight of another boat, or ship really, a bizarre sight that looked a cross between the Poole chain ferry and a World War Two landing craft.

At that moment his phone rang. 'Herr Manning, Good morning. I am Erich Shilltinberg. I understand you wish to speak with me about yachts and sailing?'

Dave was alert now and excited. 'Yes, Sir. I would be very honoured.'

'My pleasure. Please come to der Burkliplarz dock and look for the ship *Hermione* on pontoon four.'

'Thank you sir, that's where I am now.'

'Gut, *Hermione* is an unusual ship – there is none other like her.'

'Sir, I think I can see you. I was admiring your ship when you called.'

Dave could see the name now on the side of the odd craft as she backed slowly into to the dock stern on. Then a landing ramp slowly lowered to reveal a flat deck with a four-by-four car parked and an elderly man in an electric wheelchair. So, here was the reclusive Erich Shilltinberg. Dave raised a hand in recognition although he wasn't sure if this was the correct protocol. He would have to switch to, what for him, was an unusual tact. As he understood it the Swiss were a nation short on sense of humour.

The old man acknowledged the wave and beckoned. Dave walked up the metal ramp onboard the ship. Erich Shilltinberg was every bit Dave's vision of an ancient mariner apart from the wheelchair and the man's shrivelled form. He was smartly dressed but in blazer and slacks rather than a business suit. But Dave could just see the metal braces on the man's ankles. Shilltinberg held up his right arm and Dave shook hands.

The old man called out an order and two crew hands retrieved the ship's lines and gently they slid away from the dockside and out into the waters of the lake. Shilltinberg barked another order in German and a smart steward brought Dave a cane chair with a  table and a glass of laager. Suddenly Dave was beginning to enjoy this trip.

'Mr Manning,' the old man's voice was gentle but more accented than his office minion. 'Once I would have sailed and raced on these waters but it was not to be.'

'I've heard you were an Olympic sailor, sir.'

'Never so much. But as you are concerned at recent events in England I will speak with much honesty.'

Dave gulped his beer. This was wholly unexpected.

'I still love sailing and I love yachts; all sorts of yachts. But sadly I must confine myself to this power ship. I must not be what you English call, what is it? I mean one whose tales make you fall sleep.'

'I think you mean a bore, sir. But you certainly won't have that effect on me.'

Shilltinberg took a sip at his own glass. 'My quarrel with Crickerman goes back much further than today. You see we both have things that are similar, in common I think you English say. But Herr Manning are you English? I speak not your language well, but I listen and you sound different, not Yankee but are you Australian?'

The mistake happened so often that Dave no longer bristled. 'No, sir, I come from New Zealand.'

'Ah, yes a land of fine sailors and the dangerous game of ru…roo..'

'Rugby,' Dave intervened.

'Once I too might have played such a game had I not contracted the polio when I was twenty two years of age. That stopped me sailing, it stopped me from the ski slopes, it left me with no ambition but to make money and Herr Manning that believe me is no compensation.' He took a further sip from his glass. 'You understand, memories I will take with me when I go, but money I cannot. When I came here with my father and mother we had nothing.'

'I'm sorry, sir.'

'There is no need. My parents were German but they were Jewish. They did not practice religion, but this was Germany and the year was 1934. We came to this city. I was five-years-old.'

'I think I understand, sir.'

'It is so stupid. My father had hair that was blond. He would pass as an Aryan had we not been betrayed by Herman Schulz. He worked for my father and he trusted him. Schulz survived the war and although he had a bad Nazi record he manages to find his way to Australia. Am I to understand that there they play a game called Cricket?'

'Yes, we do as well and so do the English.'

'So it happens. Schulz takes the name Crickerman finds himself a wife and breeds a son who makes much money and thinks he can take it with him.'

'Sir, you mean Hengist Crickerman?'

'Yes, he is the one. Herr Manning. I speak to you because I am familiar with you. You write about the Olifa Olympics and I read you in the paper called World of Yachting?'

'I think you mean the magazine *Yachting World.*'

'Indeed, and Herr Manning you write with care, but things I can read that you do not show.'

'In England we say read between the lines, sir.'

'That is how I mean. I will be honest. I have an Olifarian associate who behaved with much badness and it cost him a big amount of his fortune.' Shilltinberg looked genuinely distressed.

Dave took a risk. 'Are we talking about Primo Garcia? I think he's staying in your house in England. You see someone who knew him recognised him.' That was as far as Dave was going to commit himself.

'You are correct. My daughter lives there and she found Garcia in Chile in much distress. He is, what you say, a naughty boy but in his time he was a fine sailor. But I do not excuse what he tried to do to those nice little girls and he did not succeed. Worse he tried to stop Simpson. He is now a Ritter or a Sir – Knight is it?'

'That's right, his Olympic double and his record in sailing did that for him. I know him and I know the three girls.'

'I wish there had been these Paralympics in my day. I would have loved a little boat like Sir Simpson's but now I am too old.'

No, thought Dave. Next time this dear old fellow comes to England I'm going to take him to Branham Lake and we'll sit him in an Access boat. He must be all of ninety but he'll die happy.

'So, Herr Manning. You have my wish that you write my story. You are a kind writer and not like others in the Daily Banner. The man Ollavasen was, how you say, a brutal, and a danger to women. Had I realised what he was I would never have employed him. That you wrote about the Atlantic Race was the truth and I will support you.'


'We've a report on the DNA,' said Inspector Marchway. 'I'm afraid there is no match to Michelle Le Bois and no match to anyone on the national data base. The skin sample was heavily tanned and weathered but was probably a younger man.'

'Any results from the murder site?' asked Superintendent Hollins.

'None whatever as yet. We don't think the murderer touched Le Bois except with the knife.'

'You know what that means.'

'Yes sir, it is likely that the victim knew the assailant.'

Hollins grimaced. 'This is turning out to be a sod. What about the Stonemans, they had a grievance against Le Bois?'

'Yes, sir. We had to do a check as a matter of form but Emily Stoneman was in London at her old legal chambers and Tom Stoneman was working in Yeovil. All with witnesses and the couple's nanny was in their house with the baby and she was with five guests all soldiers from Bovington.'

Hollins smiled. 'Don't tell the Daily Banner.'

'Sir, we've two identical killings and they would seem to be by the same hand but where's the link?'

'Yachts and their Yachties. Ollavasen was a professional yacht skipper and Le Bois hung around the sailing scene. I know that's not a lot to go on and hardly scientific but intuition sometimes works in this job as you know already.'

'I still think it may be bound up with Ollavasen's sex life. He must have made plenty of enemies: you know damaged women and vengeful men. We've definite testimony that he threw his last race for money. All in all, a pretty nasty piece of work. No great loss but of course we're not allowed to think that way.'

'Oh Garry, how many times in my career have I been tempted to say that.'

Dave Manning sipped his whisky as he trawled through the internet. Eventually he found what he was searching for. He picked up the phone and dialled a number. 'Hi here, can I speak to Colin Banshaw?'

'Oh, good evening. My name's David Manning and I'm a writer on sailing matters.' The man he was calling, a sports reporter for the paper in Plymouth asked the question that Dave had hoped not to have to answer.

'Yes,' Dave replied. 'I know, I also work for the Banner, but I thought we could share a potential story and if so I don't want to cramp your style. You've obviously heard of the Ollavasen murder. We think it may have a link to an incident in your town just before the start of the double Trans-Atlantic race.' Ah ha, the man was interested now.

Dave came to the point. 'I expect you know that Ollavasen was suspected of damaging a sail so that he could throw the race for cash. I need some info from forty eight hours after the race finished. First can you get hold of CCTV tapes from the marina and yacht club for that evening?' Dave paused, this Banshaw sounded nervous. 'Look, we know he disposed of the sail in a landfill tip. I think the cameras may have picked him up as he took it away from the yacht. If anything comes of this I will give you ten hours advance notice before I write anything for the Banner.'

Eventually Banshaw agreed. The possibility of a scoop story was too big a temptation for a provincial journalist to resist. Dave had failed to mention that there was something else that might well be on those tapes; a possible view of a murderer.

'How are you, Em?' Chloe asked. She was worried for her friend and it just wasn't fair.
Poor Emily, once again her life was blighted by outside events. It wasn't right when she had so recently found happiness with the birth of her little boy. And Peter was an angel. Holding the little guy in her arms had an unsettling effect on Chloe. Her sexuality was fixed so she could never aspire to child birth. Maybe Susanna could do the business. Susie she knew was one who swung both ways; bi-sexual was the academic term. But did that extend to actually bedding with a bloke? Something had once happened to Susie that the girl wouldn't speak about only that it involved a man. It could well have been this same Ollavasen. Yes, men, most of them, could be a frigging

nuisance.

Emily put Peter back in his cot and sighed. 'I can't mourn for that nasty bitch, and then I feel so guilty. She's gone and she can never again threaten Tom or me or little Peter.'

'Have you heard anything from the police?'

'They wanted to know where I was the day she was killed.'

Chloe was annoyed. 'Bloody cheek. They couldn't really think you did it?'

'No, it was only routine. But, Oh Chloe it is a relief to know she's not around any more. The whole thing was beginning to get to me.'

'I know, mate – we could all feel it.'

'That Michelle tried to kill my Tom. Hammersen was dithering and she screamed at him to shoot.'

Chloe was aware of the distress in Emily's expression. A nightmare had resurfaced and there was absolutely nothing that she could do to relieve her friend's pain.

'Anyway,' said Emily. 'You and your guys don't have to guard us now. But you and Susanna can stay as long as you like.'

'Thanks, but that can't be more than a couple of days. We're due for our overseas deployment next week,'

'Chlo, it's not where there's fighting going on?'

'Not this time. Intensive training sessions in Kenya but that probably means we'll be back in the war zone next year.'

'Will you stay a few more days?' Emily pleaded.

'Yeah, all right. Susie's with her folks in Kent for the weekend, so being here will be fine by me.'


Dione, get in here,' Hengist Crickerman called into the intercom.

His PA entered the office promptly and stared at him. 'How about please sometimes, Heng?'

'Ahh, come off it Dione; We're Aussies all this please and thank you is for Poms.'

'Well, we're working in Pomland – maybe they're right.'

'Forget it. Have you the report on our new store in Hampshire?'

'Yeah, the contractor faxed through a whole book of complaints; seems the locals are causing trouble.'

'That's just what I was saying. Poms, all lahdidah backward – don't know what's good for'em.'

Hengist became aware that Dione was glaring at him. 'Oh Gawd. What's biting you now?'

'Heng why did you tell that copper you spent the night with me, when I know you were down in Hampshire and nothing to do with our new site?'

'Bitch, you were listening.'

'Well, the intercom was on and I've got ears, ain't I?'

'Are you sure no one's listening right now?' He checked the switch. 'Yeah it's safe. Well I had private business to settle.'

'Of course you did. With that slimy little dingo, Michelle. She's dead now. Did you hire a hit man.'

'Dione, enough! I don't wanna' hear this crap. Go get me that report.'

She stared at him in way he hadn't encountered before. 'Yeah I reckon you might've done it and that lecherous shitehawk Ollavasen. What've you got to worry about? You're above the law – I've heard you say so.'

# *CHAPTER 16*

Back home in Bayswater, Dave Manning sat at his computer and began to write a series of articles. First for the Banner; he had clearance from Erich Shilltinberg to voice the latter's suspicions stopping short of any risk of libel from Crickerman. He had a separate article for the yachting press describing Erich's sailing career up and until the man was struck down with polio. Shilltinberg was anxious that Dave credited him with the building and part of the design of his maxi yachts. Dave was given photographs from the 1940s and some fresh ones of *Avocet*. No pictures were permitted of Erich Shilltinberg on his *Hermione*. Two hours later Dave had finished the articles and emailed them to the papers concerned. At that point Josie who had been at the kitchen table with her laptop demanded the main computer back for anther chapter in her new novel.

'I know what's bugging me,' she said. 'Why was Michelle Le Bois hiding out in Greatswood? I mean that's your friend Shilltinberg's place.'

'I agree; that's something worth finding out.'

Josie looked worried. 'You won't do anything reckless, Dave?'

'Reckless is not my scene, but listening with my ear to the ground is.'

She laughed. 'Contortionist are we?'

Dave took the tube to the Banner offices. Once there he sought out the chief crime reporter. 'Have the police said anything about the Le Bois murder?' he asked.

'No, they're stalling because they haven't a clue and that's not a pun it's literal. They're chasing their tales.'

Dave thought for a moment. 'Harry, can you find out anything about a man called Richard Halderholm. He runs a yacht charter firm at Hamble but they rent out boats on the Med and the Baltic?'

'I can if he's got criminal form, but what's he to do with all this?'

'Ollavasen tried to rape his sister in Denmark. Halderholm intervened and Ollavasen beat him up before the police could get there. It all ended with Ollavasen paying a fine that bankrupted him. Halderholm's got a record of violence in this country.'

Harry whistled. 'You could be onto something there.'

'One last thing. What do you know about an Olifarian called Garcia?'

'Yeah, gambling king but he came unstuck over the Olympics last year. Dunno' where he is now, but the Olifarians are not looking for him. He's in exile somewhere.'

'Yes, and somewhere is right here in the UK in a big house in Hampshire.'

'Jammy sod.'

'And Harry, I am going to talk to him.'

The crime reporter grinned. 'Dave, you're making a name with your exclusive interviews. Ok go and see what the guy has to say. Meanwhile I'll dig about these Halderholms.'

Once again Dave found his way to Greatswood and paused for a meal in the pub. The clientele were a mix of locals and well healed business types but the conversation was all about murder or more to the point the Le Bois murder.

'They say there's a sex-maniac on the loose,' said the landlord. 'We've had our lads patrolling the lanes but they haven't seen nowt.'

'What do the police say?' asked Dave.

'They don't tell us anything and I've got two teenage girls who could be raped and killed by this nutter. They've taken the dead girl's car away. Do you know it was in our car park? They took it on a low loader all wrapped up in plastic. And I told them it'd been in our car park a whole week before the poor little kid was murdered.'

'What do you know about that big house I can see?'

'Not much; belongs to some foreign bloke, a German they say. It could be 'im most likely, I don't trust foreigners, as for Germans – I hate 'em. My granddad was wounded in the blitz.'

Dave left it at that and finished his meal. He had his journalist ID and a copy of his Shilltinberg article so he was prepared to visit the house. His mentor Sid wouldn't have bothered. Sid's method was direct action, foot in the door, blunt questions. Well that would never work in the Shilltinberg ménage.

He walked to the iron gates and looked gloomily at the electronic security buttons, Then he saw the telephone in its little cupboard and called the number written in front of him. 'May I ask who you are and how we can help you?' The voice was so pompous it could only be a butler.

'I am a friend of Herr Shilltinberg and he has given me permission to meet his daughter Wendy.'

'Yes, Sir. Mr Shilltinberg has also informed us of this information. I will open the gates and you may proceed.' The line went dead and slowly the gates opened.

'Jeez, pompous Pom,' Dave muttered. 'What century does he think he's in?'

Dione was feeling malicious and suspicious as well and she was fed up with Hengist.

That overbearing bastard seemed to think she was a slave put there to answer his every call and whim both in the office and the bedroom. The man was rich, yes, one of the wealthiest men on the planet. Dione was a native born Aussie; her great-great how many times great grandad had been transported from England hundreds of years ago for some misdemeanour. She had never found out what he'd done but she was rather proud of him. But Hengist's dad was a German immigrant and worse, much worse, she'd been told by a journalist that the man had taken part in the Holocaust and been party to murdering children.

Hengsit couldn't help his dad, but there was something about the man: this attitude of lofty superiority. Hengist had made play for her and she had to admit he was great in bed, but what of his poor wife back in Oz. He never mentioned her. Was she even alive or had he disposed of her exactly as he probably had with Ollavasen, and more than likely with that shitty little Michelle? Would he ever face the law? But Hengist Crickerman was above the law or so he believed.

Dione walked the twenty five yards to her company apartment and took the lift to the second floor. In her bag she carried a stack of CDs and memory sticks: all secret accounts that she'd extracted from Hengist's personal files. 'Right, you sod. Let's see if I can find the hitman?' Now the doorbell was ringing triggered from the keypad in the entrance lobby.

Dione yawned and spoke into the intercom. 'Yes, who is it?'

Although the answer surprised her she was pleased. This was a caller who might know something.

'Ok, if you say so come on up.'

She opened the apartment door and waited. 'Yeah, all right, come in. You come to tell me something?' Dione turned and walked back to her desk. The knife thrust into her neck severed the jugular in one cut. Dione fell to the floor, blood gushing and gurgling into the carpet.

The Butler who opened the front door was exactly the kind of automaton that Dave had expected. 'If Sir would care to wait in the drawing room I will inform Mrs Wenman.' The man withdrew with a regal air. Dave silently mouthed an opinion at the retreating tail coat.

The room he was in was comfortable without being sumptuous. He could see furniture that might be Sheraton or that other eighteenth century maker: Chippendale; that was the one. Some of the exotic stuff had made it all the way to New Zealand. In a far corner there stood a fine grand piano: a Steinway. Dave rather prided himself on his jazz improvisations but that Butler certainly would not approve. Above the white surround of the fireplace was a portrait of a young man dressed for sailing and sitting at the tiller of a six metre class yacht. The man looked familiar until Dave suddenly realised that he was staring at the likeness of Erich Shilltinberg, but a much younger Erich in his pre-illness heyday. He moved closer.

'That is my father,' said a soft voice behind him.

He turned to see a smiling late middle-aged woman. She was dressed in jeans and flip flops with a long tailed multicoloured shirt over her top half. Dave wondered what the butler thought of this casual ensemble.

'You're David,' the woman held out her hand and he shook it. 'I'm Wendy. My father emailed us and said you might be calling. He likes you and you made quite an impression when you met in Zurich.'

Dave was baffled. Erich Shilltinberg spoke English reasonably well but with a heavy accent and odd grammar. This daughter spoke perfect English with a slight American accent. The woman must have guessed his thoughts. 'My father was struck down with polio and I regret to say it but my mother behaved disgracefully. She took me and fled to New York and for thirty years I never saw my father. Then in the nineteen seventies I found him and we've been close ever since.'

'I met your father three days ago and I liked him. I was so sorry he never achieved his Olympic dream.'

'I know. That was the disappointment that shaped his whole life.'

Wendy pointed him to an armchair and sat down opposite. 'Mr Manning, you are a journalist and that means you are not here for your health.'

Well she was certainly making it easy for him. 'Mrs Wenman…'

'No, please I'm Wendy. Wendy Wenman sounds a bit stupid but Wenman was my late husband. Now, I guess you want to know why Michelle Le Bois was here.'

Dave was shocked by her openness. 'Do the police know?'

'Not yet. Two of them turned up when she was still with us.'

Dave was alarmed. 'Look, I won't write anything until you've made a statement to the police. But you must do that.'

'Yes, I guess you're right,' she replied.

'I know I am. I'm not sure that they are getting anywhere and you may reveal something however trivial that they need to know.'

Wendy paused in thought. 'She turned up out of the blue one night. We had another guest in the house and she wanted to speak to him.'

Garcia, Dave guessed. He had often wondered if there was an Olifa connection between those two and the mad Hammersen. 'Did she tell you what it was all about?'

'No, it was all very private and our guest didn't comment but he persuaded us to let her stay for a few days. Then the police called and she fled the place and was horribly killed. You can imagine how that made us feel. Tell me, was she wanted for a crime?'

'No, not as far as I know and the police knew nothing about her until she was killed.'

Wendy looked really worried. 'Our other guest left the same day. He's Primo Garcia, and he is a bit of a rogue as I think you would say.'

'I know all about him,' said Dave. 'Is he the one who tried to sabotage the Olifa games?'

'Yes, something of the sort. My father took pity on him and helped him in exile but I doubt it was him that killed the girl. He was definitely here when this Michelle left us.'

Dave wondered. 'From what you say, he's not here now.'

'No, but he's due to return after this weekend. So the police cannot speak to him today.'

Chief Inspector Marchway received the call from the MET. The spokesman in London was a bit too patronising for his taste.

'We've had an incident on our territory and it has similarities to certain incidents which I believe you are trying your best to solve.'

'How can I help you?' Marchway gritted his teeth. Clearly this sophisticated London copper regarded him as a backward country cousin.

The London man gave a detailed report. The dead girl was Hengist Crickerman's office PA and her throat had been cut almost certainly by some person or person that she recognised.

'Crickerman?' Marchway jumped at the name. 'Then there could be a clear connection between at least one of our cases.' He gave the man a brief explanation of the Ollavasen murder and of Ollavasen's dubious connection to Crickerman. 'Mind you, I think this could be coincidence you see Ollavasen was a sexual predator, had a conviction overseas. Could be any number of people wanting him out of the way. But that includes Crickerman.'

The London man grunted. 'What about your other incident – the girl?'

'We can't find a connection with Ollavasen and none of his yacht crew know a thing about her. Can you enlighten me about your London case? As you say there may be a connection.'

'She was Dione Logan, Australian from Melbourne. Crickerman brought her with him to London six years ago. Bit more than a PA it seems. Witnesses say the relationship soured a bit lately. When we secured the crime scene we found she had a stack of Crickerman's confidential accounts on her desk.'

'That alone is suspicious.'

'Inspector, we are questioning Mr Crickerman but we are hoping to keep the press at arms length until we know more.'

Marchway replaced the phone and went outside into the fresh air. Crickerman was arrogant, he was an Australian; no that was prejudice and not fair. He could speculate but only within the facts. Crickerman was ruthless. Marchway wouldn't put it past the man to arrange for awkward persons to be removed. Ollavasen was demanding money for a very dubious match fixing. If only he could find a connection between Ollavasen, Le Bois and Crickerman then he might have a trail that could give his career a massive boost.

'So long folks,' Chloe waved cheerfully. She was attired in full uniform with her major's badges of rank and medal ribbons.

'Have a good trip,' Emily called.

'Not sure about that,' Chloe laughed. 'Twelve hours on the floor of a bloody great Hercules ain't my idea of first class travel.'

Chloe's four army colleagues had left two days before. Emily kept telling herself that she should feel guilty and not pleased, but the removal of Michelle Le Bois had been a huge relief. That woman's irrational hatreds would have made Emily question her sanity.

'Oh come on, Susie,' Chloe called. 'I'll be back. It's not for ever.'

Susanna had been alternating between laughter and tears all morning. Emily was impressed; she didn't understand the lesbian life-style but she liked the way these two depended on each other. Thank God, and maybe it was truly God who had made Emily as she was and sent her this lovely man and beautiful child.

She smiled at Susanna. 'Cheer up; we'll take you sailing if you like. We're taking Dad's *Puffin*. Dave and Josie are coming as well and it's our first chance for Peter to have a taste of sailing.

Susanna turned to her and grinned. 'Oh Emily, I'd love that – haven't been to sea since the big race. You're so kind but I don't want to be in your way though.'

'No of course you won't be in the way, but *Puffin* will be a bit of a let down after your maxi boat.'

'Don't care. I just want to be out of this and get to sea.'

Chloe had driven away. Emily gathered her unit would spend several weeks recovering broken down vehicles in the middle of the Kenyan bush; strenuous but not deadly. Emily knew that a similar mission in Afghanistan had nearly done for Chloe. Her unit had been ambushed and her soldiers had retaliated and driven off the assailants. Chloe would never talk much about this but Emily knew her men in the best sense of the word loved and trusted her.

Susanna had waved them goodbye and promised to be at Itchenor ready to board ship on Saturday. Emily went indoors to feed Peter first and then her husband. That afternoon Dave Manning and his girlfriend Josie called by.

'I've been to Greatswood House,' said Dave. 'Seems that little girl had a guilty conscience. The people there say she flitted when the police called that day and she was killed no more than half an hour later. So she flitted but only got as far as the footpath. Was someone out looking for her?'

'That's what it seems like,' said Tom.

'As far as Michelle is concerned I've got the police a really juicy suspect. Yeah our old mate Garcia.'

Tom gaped at him. 'So it really was Garcia in that house.'

'But him being there is logical. Garcia is a scoundrel but he's conned Erich Shilltinberg. You know what a charmer conman Garcia is. Erich doesn't approve of what Garcia did in Olifa, but he swears the man is reformed and his daughter who lives in the big house agrees.'

'Hey hang on, Dave. Do the police know anything about this?'

'Mrs Wenman, she's the daughter went to the police in Southampton this morning and made a statement.'

'So the connection between Garcia and Le Bois could go all the way back to the Olifa business.'

'But that wouldn't be enough for him to kill her,' said Dave. 'And it seems he was in that house and in view at the time.'

Tom put his head in his hands. 'God, what is it about us people that these things follow us around?'


'Oh come on, Mum. It's perfectly safe,' Emily groaned. 'Look, when we get to Itchenor, Tom and Dave will take the inflatable and go get the boat. We three girls plus Peter wait on the pontoon and board the ship there. And of course Peter's coming. It'll be his first taste of sailing.'

'It sounds sensible enough to me,' said her father. 'We took you for a sail when you weren't much older.'

'I know,' Kirsten smiled. 'I fuss too much.'

'That's settled then,' said Steve. 'Wait there and I'll get *Puffin's* sails.'

'We've got hold of a little carrycot,' Emily continued. 'Peter can sleep in that in the cockpit if it's warm or down below when it gets chilly.'


Two hours later they were afloat and sailing. Some early mist and light rain had cleared and all five adults were revelling in the conditions of light to moderate wind and warm late July sunshine. Peter had been asleep and oblivious in his cot on the cockpit floor until Emily had needed to give him a feed. Down below was safer anyway away from the feet of her companions each time the ship was tacked.

'What class of boat is this?' Susanna asked.

'She's not a racing machine,' Tom explained. 'She's a Hunter Horizon 27-foot. Emily's dad bought her for cruising around locally, but Em and me borrowed her for a trip down west to Duddlestone. That's when we really got to know each other. You know a boat does that sometimes.'

'Oh really,' Emily called out from the cabin. 'My mum says every man becomes a brute the moment he steps aboard a boat.'

'Like that bastard Ollavasen,' said Susanna.

Tom looked at her with annoyance. 'Hey, I don't like that comparison. Come on, Susie. It's a lovely day and he's dead.'

'Had it coming,' Susanna muttered.

'You may be right from what we've heard,' said Dave. Who was steering.

'My Chloe would have been a better skipper and she wouldn't have been bought. With her they'd've won.'

'I can't argue with that,' said Tom.

The gloomy talk couldn't deflate their mood for long. The wind had increased a couple of knots and Tom decided to pull down a reef in the mainsail. That called for everyone's attention for the next five minutes. They settled down for a long reaching leg out towards Bembridge.

'Let's take a look at the Nab,' said Emily as she emerged on deck again. 'Peter's asleep I think he likes the ship's motion.'

'Another Olympic medal winner?' said Dave.

'Maybe,' Emily laughed 'Who can tell.'

'I like the big boats,' said Susanna 'Emily, you were fantastic but I was never much use in dinghies.'

'I've done both,' said Dave. 'Wasn't much use in either. Them as can do and them as can't write about it.'

'I love this boat of yours,' said Josie. 'She seems to have everything under control herself. I've never felt so relaxed under sail before.'

It was true thought Tom. The little Hunter was a superb all rounder. She could stand anything the English Channel could throw at her and be safe and have a fair turn of speed as they had right now.'

'Hengist's talking of building a new yacht even bigger than *Qualistores,*' said Susanna. 'I'm getting a place in her crew come what may.'

'Well you did a good job for him in the last race,' said Tom.

'Trouble is that navigator is about the only place for a girl. All the skippers want macho blokes to wind winches.'

'Chloe can do that Ok,' laughed Emily.

They reached the area of the Nab Tower. The odd looking structure had always intrigued Tom. His step-father, the other Peter, had told him that it was built in the first war under such maximum secrecy that when hostilities ceased no one knew what it was for. So it was towed out here and placed as the most easterly light on the approaches to Spithead and the Solent.

'Still a fair tide for home,' said Tom. 'I think we'll turn round now, go home and have a good meal in the pub.'

The food in the Inn at Itchenor was good plain fair. Three courses washed down with a couple of bottles of a local Sussex wine, while Peter enjoyed his milk. Tom and Dave as the car drivers had had to restrict themselves to one glass of the wine. They were all happy and content. There had been one surprise. To Dave's eyes a remarkably pretty girl had served them their food. Susanna had left them to go to the toilet and the rest of the party were about to carry their drinks outside.

Emily had become excited. 'Hi, Nicky,' she called. 'Nicky Coulden. It is you isn't it?'

'Emily,' the waitress girl grinned and rushed forward to embrace her. 'I've read all about you and your gold medal. And I saw you win on the telly. Well done!'

Emily turned to the others, 'Nicky and I were at school together just up the road in Chichester.' She turned to her friend. 'Nicky, do you still sail?'

'You bet. I've got an instructor's ticket and I've done some big boat stuff in Australia three years ago.' She dropped her voice. 'I'm working here for the summer and doing some other jobs on the side. Me and my boyfriend want to buy our own boat.'

'Do we know him, or is he still the same one?' Emily grinned mischievously.

'What, Jason? Yeah, you've met him. He's got his full yachtmaster ticket now and he skippers for Mulberry at Hamble.'

Dave sat up in surprise. 'So does, Ed Coulden, I met him in Plymouth.'

'Sure, he's my brother. Was that after the trans Atlantic race?'

'Yes.'

'You must be Dave the writer. You sound New Zealand by the way you talk.'

'Thank you for that, Nicky. You've no idea how irritating it is when everyone thinks you're an Aussie.'

'I wasn't happy about Ed crewing for Crickerman, that man is a prize shit, excuse my French, but I suppose that's better than taking orders from Ollavasen on that other boat. I'm glad he's dead and gone for ever. It would be nice if Crickerman was to join him.'

'Steady on…' said Emily.

'All right I withdraw that. It's just that I saw the worst side of that guy is Australia.'

'What do you do these days, Nicky?' asked Emily. 'Do you work in sailing full time?'

'No, worse luck but Jason does. No, in the week I work for Yachting Global International. Before you ask I don't write anything, I just answer the phone and fetch and carry for the editor.' Nicky looked around nervously. 'Emily, there's something I need to tell you in private. I've been wondering for weeks whether I should contact you.'

Emily frowned at the others.' Could you guys wait here a minute, please?' She followed her friend out of the pub into the sunshine. She returned on her own three minutes later looking disconsolate.

'What was that all about, Em?' Tom asked.

'It's odd,' said Emily. 'But it seems Michelle Le Bois cornered Nicky and her Jason and poured out a whole lot of shit against me. Good for Nicky she blazed back and this Jason went further. He threatened Michelle with violence and that's what worries Nicky.'

Emily sank into a despondent silence. Susanna came back in the room and looked oddly at Emily and shook her head. 'What did Nicky tell you about me?'

Emil's looked startled. 'She never mentioned you. Why should she?'

'I saw her when we came in and I avoided her. She knows things about Hengist that make him look bad.'

The only other odd moment came when Dave picked up a copy of the Daily Banner.

SUPERMARKET BOSS GIRL STABBED.

Silently Dave held up the paper and showed them the headline; for a few seconds it brought all five of them down to earth.

'The police haven't released a name,' said Dave. 'I can't say if it's our man that's involved.'

'Nah, that one, she never came near us on the boat,' Susanna muttered. 'Waste of space.'

'Come on,' said Emily. 'We're here to forget all that sort of stuff. I'll get the bill and we'll divide the cost by five.'

'Don't ask Dave to do that,' Josie giggled. 'He's hopeless at maths.'

Detective Chief Inspector Marchway arrived at the headquarters building of Qualistores International to meet Detective Inspector Wallace of the Metropolitan Police. The MET had not been deferential but had virtually ordered Hangist Crickerman to be available at nine thirty. The man had failed to greet them with good cheer, which was hardly surprising and beneath a blustering exterior Marchway detected nervousness.

'All right, somebody's topped the silly little bimbo – boyfriend most likely. Don't ask me. How should I know?'

'Were you aware, sir,' asked Wallace, 'that the young lady had a stack of your confidential financial files on her desk?'

Crickerman clearly did not know and for the first time his eyes conveyed alarm. 'She was my confidential PA. I guess she took them home to work late. She was a good, yes a very good worker. I'll hand that to her.'

'Now, sir, perhaps you would care to describe your movements on the night in question?'

'I sat in here and put a couple of calls back home to Melbourne and then I went to bed.'

'Thank you, sir. We can of course trace your calls but can you tell us what time you did as you say go to bed and where would that be?'

'It was ten thirty and I went to my apartment in this building.' Crickerman began to bluster again. 'Look, I didn't kill her. She was a good PA. I'm going to have one hell of a job replacing her.'

'Very well, sir. We may discuss this again so do not leave the building.'

Crickerman bristled and his face reddened. 'Nobody tells me what to do in my own office.'

'Did Miss Logan order you around?' asked Marchway. 'Did she defy you once too often?'

'Look copper, I'm not answering any more questions without my lawyer present. Got that?'

They left the office with Crickerman sitting behind his desk looking visibly crumpled.

'He did it,' said Wallace.

'What all three murders?'

'Can't say about your killings but hell; he looked bloody guilty to me.'

In the entrance hall they found three uniformed officers and some very nervous reception staff. 'We got'em,' said a constable. 'All the CCTV tapes from that evening.' He held up a large plastic bag.

Outside the building a large crowd bystanders had gathered. It was the height of the business hour and these people seemed to have nothing better to do than gawp.

'We'll look at the dead girl's flat,' said Wallace. 'It's only just round the corner.'

They reached the plush apartment block and entered the front door. A police tape had been strung a few yards from the building and behind it crammed fourteen press photographers.

'I call this a lobby,' said Wallace. 'But on the detail it says "the keypad is in the vestibule"; very posh. Doesn't quite fit with Qualistores. My Missus shops there. Pile it high and sell it cheap. I don't like Australians – too gobby for their own good.'

'We beat them at cricket,' said Marchways.

Wallace was examining the buttons on the entry key system. 'No prints – we've already checked and nothing on the lift buttons either.'

'Planned and pre-meditated then,' said Marchways.

'And nothing in the flat. Looks like the victim knew her killer.'

'That's exactly the same as our second killing in Hampshire.'

Wallace turned and nodded. 'Michelle Le Bois. Yes, our computer records turned up some things about her. She did time in France, got herself expelled from Olifa during the Olympics and she threatened those little girlies who won gold in the boats.'

Despite the seriousness of the investigation Marchway smiled at the idea of Chloe Te Koote as a "little girlie".

'Forensic can't find anything in here,' said Wallace as he examined the interior of the lift. He pulled on his own gloves before pressing the ascent button.

The body had long since been removed but an ugly darks stain was still visible on the carpet. But it was a dull place, thought Marchway: no pictures and nothing but Sixties tube and plastic furniture. He pulled on his own gloves and examined the desk.

'We've taken all the tapes and discs, said Wallace. 'They may be relevant. Could be Crickerman wanted to stop her passing on sensitive info.'

In that case he would have departed with the files himself. Crickerman was certainly capable of disposing of inconvenient people but surely he would arrange for a hitman to do a cleaner job in much less obvious place. Crickerman was linked to two murders: Ollavasen and now Dione Logan. Intuition for a police detective could be dangerous but somewhere there was a link to the death of Michelle Le Bois. Did Wallace know about the helicopter trip?

'Inspector, did you know that Crickerman took a helicopter ride into my territory on the night of the Ollavasen murder and the helicopter returned here to city airport with no Crickerman just the pilot.'

'How did you know all that?' Wallace the Scotland Yard man was clearly irritated by this smug country cousin.

'City Airport log all movements. The pilot deposited a passenger list but no flight plan. He landed at an airfield on my patch and not far from Hamble where Ollavasen was knifed.'

'Did you tell us you were mucking around on our ground?'

'The questions were asked by my governor: Chief Superintendent Hollins and I imagine he talked to one of you commissioners first.' So sod you smug MET copper, Marchway smiled to himself.

Dave Manning took the surprise phone call at breakfast. 'Ah, Mr Manning I do hope I have not unduly surprised you.'

It was a vaguely familiar voice but who the hell?

'I'm Waterborne.'

Are you indeed, thought Dave. What nutter have we here?

'Yes, I am Mr Shilltinberg's maitre de maison at Greatswood. You paid us a visit recently.'

'Oh, you're the butler.' Dave recalled the strange automaton at the big house. 'Yes, I remember. How can I help you?'

'Sir, I know that Mr Shilltinberg regards you highly. I have certain information that I think you should be aware of. I have communicated by telephone with Mr Shilltinberg and he felt you were the person I should speak with.'

'Very well, Mr Waterborne. What is it you want to say?'

'I would much prefer, sir that we meet face to face before I impart such sensitive material.'

'All right. I admit I'm at a loose end for the rest of today. Where do you want to meet me?'

'I shall be off duty the whole of this current afternoon. I can recommend this café in Alresford. It is a nice discreet venue and I do not believe anyone there will recognise us.'

'All right, Mr Waterborne. I know the place. I've friends who live nearby.'

Dave was feeling more than a little shell-shocked when he called at Tom and Emily's cottage. He had phoned through to them the moment he finished his meeting with the incongruous Waterborne in the café in Alresford High Street. The interview had been heavy going, but Dave liked this little English town with its picture book architecture and quaint little shops. It was in one of these that he had paused long enough to buy some colour postcards to send to his folks back home.

'Come on in, Dave,' said Emily. 'Kettle's on and I've fed the boy.'

She ushered him into the kitchen and he settled himself on a stool by the table.

'Tom's in Yeovil again,' she said. 'What's more I've been back at work for the first time since the birth.'

'Well done,' Dave sipped his tea. After an hour of Mr Waterborne this was nectar.

'Yes, I'm due to prosecute a couple of teenage idiots who stole a lorry and smashed it into a public toilet near Reading.'

Dave laughed. 'That doesn't sound like a profitable ram raid.'

'They're both over eighteen so it's full court appearance for them but they've already done time in a young offender's jail.'

Dave drained the rest of his cup and Emily filled it again. 'I've just had a talk to a guy called Waterborne. He's the butler at Greatswood Manor. Jeez I thought Poms like him went out with Noel Coward.'

'Why, is he gay?'

'No, I would guess the guy is a neuter if he ever had any private life.'

Emily laughed. 'Well, Dave I'm not going to put you through a cross examination but you've got me intrigued. Do tell all.'

'You know I'm beginning to feel I'm the detective in all this. Somehow since I saw dear old Erich Shilltinberg I seem to be one jump ahead of the police.'

Emily looked worried. 'You must tell them what you know.'

'Oh I do and I will, in my own good time, but I'm not sure they take much notice. To them I'm just a daft Antipodean reporter.'

'I'm not sure about that. I know from my work that the police value information from the press. You see the fictional idea of one devoted copper hounding down his criminal isn't quite true. They've probably got a hundred unsolved cases and they do need people like you who hear things.'

'Trouble is, most of my findings are speculative like today's. This

Waterborne claims he went for a walk in the grounds and he saw Michelle talking with a strange man actually on the footpath where she was killed. Apparently this was a week or so before she was killed there. Well, Mr Waterborne moves around like a wraith, I know I've seen him. Anyway he reckons he could identify the strange man, but I'm a bit doubtful because he's only seen him speaking on the telly.'

'Waterborne,' Emily sniggered. 'He can't really be called that can he?'

'So he says, why?'

'Next time I have a kid it's going to be a waterbirth. I'm told it's quite relaxing and the bloody dry land version hurts like hell. You've no kids have you?'

'No, Josie wants them. She's gone all broody since she met you and Peter. We're getting married in Auckland sometime around Christmas and then we'll see.'

'Oh Dave that's fantastic. Can we come?'

'Too right you're coming. We want you and Chloe as bridesmaids.'

'Ok we're on, but I'm so sorry, Dave. You didn't finish about Mr Waterbirth.'

'Waterborne, past tense. The point is he thinks that the stranger was Crickerman but he doesn't know the man and he's only seen him in the TV interviews after the Atlantic race. Two things: this was the evening that Michelle turned up at the house and Waterborne reckons she was in one hell of a state, all trembling and crying, and do you guess which day that was?

'Dave, I'm a lawyer not a clairvoyant. What day?'

'It was all within an hour or two of Ollavasen's murder and not twenty miles away. I had a covert talk to one of the forensic blokes and he says there was DNA evidence but it didn't match Michelle or anyone on the national data base. I wonder if they've got round to testing Hengist Crickerman?'

'Dave, do you know why Michelle was at Greatswood?'

'Waterborne said she'd come to see Garcia. Seems it was urgent and she was, as I say in one hell of a state or so the Butler claims.'

Shortly afterward Dave had finished his third cup of tea and relieved himself in the downstairs toilet, Tom arrived home. 'Cup of tea, my angel. I've had one hell of a day.

What was yours like, Dave?'

Dave told him everything he'd already told Emily.

'Crikey, seems all these weird people are telling you what they won't tell the cops.'

'That often happens in journalism.'

'We're well out of it now and I intend to see it stays that way. But you can be our detective and keep us posted.'

Dave was in two minds about his next question but it was something that had bothered him since the weekend. 'You remember we had that great meal in the Ship at Itchenor?'

'Of course it rounded off a good day. Got all of us away from all this shit.'

'Do you remember I found a copy of that day's Daily Banner. I will have to check with them, but I thought the London police were keeping the lid on the girl Logan and Crickerman to avoid sensation. So how did the Banner get hold of the story? None of the other sheets did.'

'I must say that was the first we'd heard about it,' said Tom. 'Could they have found out by phone hacking the police?'

'No way. We've all been warned off that. Not even the Banner would risk it now.'

There was something else also bothering Dave about the same incident. Another of those irritating things, he mused, that failed to add up.

# CHAPTER 19

'Garry, I will have to reduce your manpower on these murders.' Superintendent Hollins looked suitably gloomy.

'I must admit sir, we're getting nowhere. My gut feeling is that the murders are linked but we can't work purely on intuition.'

'That is so very true. The crime rate is as high as ever.'

'I know, sir. We've had four violent breaking and entries, two armed robberies, two arson, and a couple of other suspicious deaths, let alone all the usual problems.'

'Is there anything new you can give me on the Ollavasen case?'

'Yes, sir. We've a list of the calls Ollavasen made with his mobile phone. There were two calls to Hengist Crickerman's home number. Both only lasted seconds and it looks likely they were dictated to answer machines.'

'Well, Garry that's better than nothing.'

'Yes, sir, we've told the MET and given them the dates so they will check the tapes. Most likely Crickerman deleted anything embarrassing though.'

'I've talked to the producers of Crimewatch,' said Hollins. 'But our evidence is all too vague. The CCTV wasn't working when Ollavasen was killed and we've no idea how Michelle Le Bois came to be on that footpath. It's even worse for the MET. The CCTV at Dione Logan's flat was also inactive.'

'If it's all right, sir. I'd like to make a direct appeal to the public. Somebody must have seen something. That footpath runs near a couple of farm yards both are a long way from the crime scene but somebody may have seen walkers and remembered them.'

'Turn on the news, Em,' Tom called from the bathroom..

'Turn it on yourself. I'm in the bloody kitchen.'

'I'm in the shower.'

'Well get out of it and go turn the telly on. I'm cooking.'

Tom slipped out of the cascade and reached for his towel. Of course Emily would never bother to drape herself in any towel. Frankly he had not enjoyed the warm days this summer while sanctimonious neighbours had made snide comments after Emily had started nude sunbathing again. At least she was keeping little Peter well covered.

He yawned and pressed the remote. Five second later he had a shock.



The presenter in the studio began a long interrogation of a crime reporter standing beside the Scotland Yard rotating sign.

*'Scotland Yard will make no comment as to whether they are also questioning Mr Crickerman about complicity in the murder of his secretary, Dione Logan. We anticipate a big fall in the share prices of Qualistores International.'* The crime reporter tilted his head and stared at the camera in what Tom assumed he thought was his most captivating pose.

Emily was standing in the doorway her mouth hanging open. 'You'd better ring Dave,' she said.

As if by some sort of sensory perception the telephone was already ringing and the caller was Dave Manning. 'Can't tell you folks that much as the law are playing it pretty close but the Banner's crime chief had a word with them. Seems the girl Dione had a compromising answerphone tape and there's messages on it from Ollavasen.'

'Threatening messages?' asked Tom.

'Must've been if the police pulled Crickerman in for that. Probably Crickerman was stalling on paying the bribe money. I've already told the cops to find that crewman I told you about – the one calling himself, Ed.'

'That'll probably be Eddie Coulden,' said Emily into the extension phone. 'He used to work for my Dad and I was at school with his sister; you know Sammy the one in the pub at Itchenor.'

'That's the guy. Seems he works for the Mulberry yacht charter firm. I'm trying to find this girl the one Ollavasen attacked in Denmark. When I've news I'll contact you.'

'Thanks, Dave.'

Tom glanced back at the television but the news had moved on to events elsewhere.

Emily walked back in the room stopped and suddenly let fly a cackle of laughter. A bit out of place, Tom thought. Then she pointed at him and laughed again. Now he saw why. His towel had slipped to the floor and he was standing there stark naked. Then the wretched girl stooped, grabbed the towel and fled upstairs giggling like a ten-year-old.

'Nice of the MET to tell us after they've told the bloody tabloids,' said Inspector Marchway. He was addressing a morning briefing of his reduced incident team.

'Sir,' asked his sergeant. 'Can we see the transcripts of these phone messages?'

'Hang on, son. I can do better than that. I have audio copies and this one is the key.'

He had already inserted the CD copy that the courier had delivered that morning. He pressed start. The voice was distorted, the accent foreign and its grasp of English sketchy.

*'You say you pay when our boat loses. When are you going to keep the deal?'*

'That's the first message,' said Marchway. 'Doesn't tell us any more than that there was something dodgy going on. Now message two.

*'Ok, I leave you bloody message. You pay up or I tell the world you are fucking scoundrel.'*

'Forty eight hours later the man was dead.'

The sergeant looked disappointed. 'Then that's it. The supermarket guy did it.'

'No it's not that easy. There's no match between Crickerman and the DNA sample from the victim's hand.'

'So he paid someone to do his dirty work?'

'In that case it wasn't a very clean job. A contract killer would have killed somewhere less public and we'd never have seen the body again.'

Marchway had already taken a decision that he hoped he would not live to regret. 'The MET can try and connect Mr Crickerman to this crime if they like. It is my opinion that this killing could have a connection to Ollavasen's sex life. Forensic say that scrap of skin is tiny but they think it's enough to work on. Doesn't mean it'll match any DNA on our registers.' He looked at his reduced team: just three plain clothes officers and a uniform WPC. 'First, trace all the crew members of both the yachts involved and find out all you can about Ollavasen's private life. From what the Danish police tell me it was pretty dire. So, go to it and good luck.'

The team dispersed except for the WPC. 'Sir?'

'Yes Constable, what is it?'

'It's that journalist, Sir, called Manning. He says he has a witness we should talk to.'

The same afternoon Inspector Wallace was briefing his much larger investigation team.

Crickerman was being held in a police station not far from Canary Wharf. The man was behaving to type. He varied between bluster, threats, and complete non-cooperation. This didn't impress Wallace. He had got his man it was only a question of proof. He needed time to secure that proof and he was not going to be mucked about by expensive lawyers and even less by the Home Office, the Foreign Office and the Australian High Commission. It seemed that the arrest had created shock and outrage in some sections of Australian society. Apparently this entrepreneur pirate was admired and many felt he was being persecuted for being an Aussie by snobbish prejudiced Brits. Then not ten minutes ago he had received a huge missing piece in the jigsaw. Hampshire Force had come up with the goods.

'Gentlemen, ladies. We have a witness statement from Hampshire police. Hengsit Crickerman was seen in contact with Michelle Le Bois at a house in Hampshire twenty miles from the murder site on the night of the murder of Alfred Ollavasen.' Wallace paused to let his words sink in to the group. Even as he spoke he had begun to have doubts. Marchway, his contact, had not been convinced. The butler, Waterborne, had never seen Crickerman for real and the appearance of Michelle Le Bois was adding an additional complication.

'Do we think that Crickerman was responsible for three murders?' An irritating woman sergeant was asking the question he hadn't wanted to answer.

'At the moment there is nothing to connect the Le Bois case to the two murders we are investigating.'

It only complicated matters that the butler served a house owned by Erich Shilltinberg the owner of the sabotaged yacht. What was Le Bois doing there and what was Crickerman doing there? For heaven's sake Crickerman and Shilltinberg were the adversaries in this libel case. Along with the uproar from Australia this case was not doing his promotion prospects much good.

'Sir, the sergeant persisted. Does this witness know Crickerman personally?'

This stupid bitch was too sharp by half. 'Mr Crickerman is a familiar figure in the press and on television,' he replied.

'Sir, could you play the answerphone messages again?' asked another officer.

Wallace obliged and even as he pressed the start button he mused what he had thought all day. If this helped convict Crickerman he would have to share the credit with Hampshire. That was as maybe and anyway the tabloids were far more interested in poor Dione.


'How did it all go?' asked Tom.

'It was almost too easy,' said Emily.

'So you put the two yobs away then?'

'Prison's too good for them sorts,' said Lily as she handed baby Peter to Emily.

'Well prison is what they've got,' said Emily 'Eighteen months although if they behave they'll be out well before that.'

'Then it'll be robbery and murder, you mark my words.'

'Lily you are a pessimist,' Emily laughed happily as she cuddled her son. 'But you've a point. They've got to improve the way they re-educate youngsters like that so they don't come out and go straight back to crime.'

'How would you feel if you were prosecuting in a murder trial?' asked Tom.

'That's my job or it will be when I've more experience. The point is you present the facts as facts and let the jury decide. I must say I'm glad we've gone past the days of hanging for murder. I wouldn't have liked prosecuting then.'

Tom was happy because Emily was clearly happy to be back at work in the career where she shone. Already she had put down a few spectacular markers for the future starting with that trial in Winchester just before she left for Olifa. Memory of that made Tom uneasy. The man who had committed perjury, Smidgin, had subsequently been given two years although Emily had had no part in that trial. Smidgin was still languishing in Ford Prison and with remission was due out any time soon. In jail he had threatened revenge on Emily. The police had been supportive but Tom still worried.

'Hey, Emily called. There's an email from Chloe. She's arrived in

Nairobi and wants Susie to find something for her.'

'Oh does she.' Tom replied. 'All these gays coming out of the woodwork everywhere.'

'I know, I know. Let's cut all this public school homophobia.'

Tom laughed at the rebuke. 'I thought you said I was the only public school type you'd ever met who wasn't one of them.'

'No, you're a full blooded hetro and I wouldn't swap you.'


Inspector Marchway was ready to go home. All was suddenly quiet on the crime front particularly since his detectives had returned to general duty. His wife was cooking a roast tonight and then he would have a comfortable few hours in front of the telly. He scowled as a bleep came on his intercom. 'Harper, Forensic Surgeon, I've some inform-ation for you.'

Well be quick about it, Marchway muttered inwardly. Harper was the man in charge of the morgue; the one who had the delightful task of cutting up the corpses. 'Go ahead.'

'It's that body of the woman Le Bois. It may be trivial but you ought to know. She's got a series of what look like serial numbers tattooed on her right arm. Can't make them out but my assistant thinks they could be bank details.'

'This is better,' Kirsten called out. 'I've had a call from Erich Shilltinberg's agent and they want us to make a complete set of sails for *Avocet.*

They were both in the main officer at Easterbroke sails. 'I'm glad someone's still got confidence in us,' Steve replied. In fact he was being unnecessarily gloomy. Business had not been unduly affected by the torn sail affair.

'Cheer up,' said Kirsten. 'We're talking big money here.'

'I know. It's not that. I'm worried about Emily. The man Smidgin is coming out of jail in a few days.'

'I know that, but Tom's contacted the police again.'

'I think they should come back to our house with the baby.'

Kirsten spun round in her office chair. 'I'd love them all to come for a few days maybe when the man comes out, but they've their own home and careers.'

'I know,' Steve sighed. 'I just don't know what the world is coming to. It seems that Crickerman's a murderer and I thought he was a great offshore skipper.'

Kirsten laughed. 'So, all your top yachties must be as pure as the driven snow. If Crickerman hadn't bribed Alfred this would never have happened.'

Steve had no reply to that. There had been something about Ollavasen that was unsettling. He couldn't put his finger on what but Steve had detected a closet violence not far below the surface. And it looked as it the sail tampering was proved fact, but tying it to Crickerman was academic since the man was in much bigger trouble.

Kirsten changed the subject. 'Steve, when Chloe was here last, did she leave an envelope with a CD in it?'

Steve remembered. 'Yes, as a matter of fact she did. It's that one from Olifa, remember, with the TV interviews with the girls and the medal ceremony. We've got our own copies but she wanted us to look after her one.'

'That's right. Chole's girl friend Susanna called and asks if it's here. I've found it and she's coming over to fetch it. If I'm not around it's in the right hand filing cabinet top drawer.'

'Bit of a waste that. Pretty little thing; pity's she's a les.'

'Oh yes,' Kirsten glared with mock severity. 'You heard from Maria lately?'

This was a sore point. Steve had had a mild infatuation with this lovely Olifarian dinghy racer. Kirsten had used this memory as a weapon ever since.

Steve sighed. 'We heard the other day, remember. She's marrying that Argentine oil baron sometime this autumn.'

'Talking about Chloe,' said Kirsten. 'I've heard that she's getting the command of one of the army's big offshore yachts.'

'I know, and she'll be good at it. She'll be a really ferocious skipper now her match racing crew have broken up.' Steve was not sure yet whether he should worry that Emily had lost interest in competitive sailing, but she did have the baby and a busy career to follow. Erin the third member of the gold medal team was teaching in Canada.

'I'll turn the radio on,' said Kirsten. 'Let's see if they've charged that Crickerman bloke.'

The Commissioner's expression was one of kindly gloom. Inspector Wallace feared the worst and he was right.

'I'm sorry, Inspector but the Crown Prosecution Service do not accept that you've enough evidence to charge this man. It's all speculation and an unreliable witness statement.'

'But, Sir,' Wallace pleaded. 'He was in that locality on the night of the murder. I'm sure if our witness saw him for real he would confirm it. And maybe it was a contract killing.'

'I'm sorry, Wallace, but we've had our experts trawling through the man's accounts and we've located every last pound he spent and even his offshore hoarding: it's all legit. I'm very sorry but you've run out of time. Release the man on police bale and make him surrender both his passports.'

Wallace was stunned; almost he felt like crying. 'Sir, he did it. He must have done it and one way or another I'm going to get him for it.'

The commissioner almost had a smile. 'There is another murder that could be connected: Michelle Le Bois.'

'No, sir, that's Hampshire's business.'

'Maybe but the name Le Bois awoke some bad memories for me and my older colleagues. We once had a police cadet of that surname in Brentford in the late seventies. Much later he was an investigating officer with Sussex Police.'

The commissioner's manner had become intense. 'The man was

under pressure and he became obsessed. He had a suspect whom he personally disliked and he tried to fit facts to back his scenario while all the time the real culprits were free and conspiring. Le Bois eventually lost it, had a total breakdown and he died in action when special-forces took out the real criminals. They were a mad cult who planned to sacrifice a small child.'

'Yes, Sir; I seem to have heard tell of this years ago. But I'm not like that. I just know that Crickerman caused that murder. No one else had any shred of motive.'

'We don't know that. I've seen stranger things. Look, go ahead and find definite proof or see what other leads come up. You never know what can happen. It's a wicked world and I mean that word for real, not street speak.'


'How do you feel about this Christening malarkey?' asked Tom.

'I like it. It'll be a nice family gathering just like the wedding,' Said Emily as she poised the bottle in Peter's mouth.

'It's all this religion thing,' said Tom. 'I know you've always been a bit of a holy roller but I don't buy it.'

He only knew that Emily had had some sort of spiritual experience years ago when she was abducted and threatened with violent death. His parents were occasional church goers. Emily's mum and dad were neutral in the matter and Emily's half sister, Sarah, was a practicing Catholic. In this matter he had to tread carefully or rather leave the decision to Emily.

'I've spoken to the vicar in South Marshall and he's up for it,' said Emily. 'We've got to give him a firm date and it could be a group thing with other families.' She smiled happily. 'Once he's done this little guy, he'll be ready to Christen our next one and the one after that.'

'Hey, wait a minute. Who said we were into breeding a whole litter?'

'Well, why not; poor little Peter will need a sister and a brother perhaps?'

'I think we should wait until all this murder business is settled.'

'Oh come on, Tom. You said we can keep out of all that. With that Michelle gone we're not involved.'

'We still know people connected to it. We sail at Hamble, we know some of the people on those big yachts that raced the Atlantic.'

'I know,' said Emily. She put down the empty bottle. 'Personally I found Susie an awful bore when she was here even if she did help out that time. Your turn next to do nappy drill,' she grinned. 'Give it another quarter of an hour.'

'Ok no problem. I'm used to it now. Tell you why I'm worried about the murders.
I heard the news on my car radio just now. The London police have released Crickerman on bale.'

'I know it was on the TV. It's police bale which means he's restricted and they can call him back any time.'

'Do you think he did it?'

'Hell, I don't know. I'm a barrister not a copper. But why should he kill Michelle?'

'He must have done.'

'No, Tom, no, no! I'm a barrister and I won't condemn anyone without conclusive proof.'

'Well, you demonstrated that in the Smidgin case.'

She sighed. 'Now that's coming back to haunt me. The police told me he's going to be out in three days time. The man's been told to stay clear of us and the police offered me a lifeline phone.'

'A what?'

'It's what they give people who've been threatened. It's usually for damaged wives and rape victims. It's a hotline special phone. All you have to do is press a pendant button and that alerts the police.'

'That sounds great.'

'I know, but I'm not sure it's for me. Smidgin is all mouth. When it comes to it I doubt he'll do anything.'

'I'm not sure about that. You not only put him away. You made him look a prize idiot and his business in Hamble went bust afterwards.'

'Well he dropped himself in the shit. I only did what I'm paid to do.'

Tom kicked off his shoes and dropped into his armchair. 'Dave rang me on my mobile. Something's bugging him about that sailing trip we did with him and Josie and Susanna.'

'I thought it was good fun, you know a day to get away from trouble.'

'I cannot make out what it is that's bothering Dave. He's not being very forthcoming. I gather someone said or did something in the pub when we were having that meal.'

Emily frowned. 'It's a popular pub with sailors and the place was packed. Apart from Nicky Coulden I didn't see anyone I knew, but maybe Dave did.'

'He's being every inch the detective and the bloody Daily Banner are encouraging him.'

'Come on it's nappy time again. Let's hope all this trouble will blow over soon.'

Tom was not convinced. 'We can only hope.'

# CHAPTER 21

Dave Manning strode into his apartment whistling cheerfully.

Josie his partner glared at him.' Do you have to?'

'Have to what?' His smile vanished. He could see that his girl was annoyed about something and it wasn't his whistling. 'Ok, what's up?'

'I've had a strange woman on the phone who wants to talk to you.'

Dave sighed. 'Strange? Do you mean the lady is a weirdo or just that you don't know her?'

'I don't know her and I was hoping that you don't either.'

'I can't answer that until you tell me her name and what she wants.'

Josie's face relaxed and now she grinned. 'I'm sure you are innocent. Her name is Sophie Evans and she wants your advice on a delicate matter.'

'The hell she does. As I've never heard of anyone with that name I'm not sure my advice'll be much use.'

Josie was laughing. 'You should have seen your face just now.'

'I haven't got a mirror in here so that would be hard.'

'Never mind, she's left a number for you to ring back.'

Dave loosed his bombshell. 'How would you fancy a trip to Australia?'

'Eh, when?'

'Next week. The Banner are paying for me to go to Melbourne and they say you can come too – all expenses paid.'

'I've never been to Australia and I wouldn't trust you to behave on your own. What's this all about?'

'The Banner reckon the solution to the Crickerman affair is in Oz and they want me to go ask questions.'

'But why you?'

'Because strange though it may seem I'm in high favour. They like the way I cracked open Shilltinberg and my interview with that dopy butler at Greatswood, although they can't print anything in it.'

'Yeah you did well.'

'And I'm not a Pom. I'm a Kiwi which isn't quite as bad. The Aussies like Crickerman and they sort of think the Poms are deliberately persecuting the man because he's been successful. As a Kiwi I'm regarded as neutral.'

Joise left her computer desk and threw her arms around him. 'Oh, Dave, my darling. You're an exciting man to be around. When do we go?'

'Monday next week. Now if you'll pass me that phone and the number I'll ring this Sophie.' He punched in the number and waited. 'Hello I| want to talk to Sophie Evans.'

It was a pleasant cultured voice that spoke. 'Oh, Mr Manning I need advice.'

'Ok, how can I help?'

'Someone gave me your name and said they thought you could help before we go to the police.'

'Hold on a minute. Who was this?'

'I can't tell you that, I promised I wouldn't. But it's my husband I'm worried about. He's the one who discovered the body of that Michelle girl near Greatswood. He's seen the new police appeal on the television and he's remembered things…'

Dave interrupted. 'Then I can't help. He's got to talk to the police.'

'I know, he doesn't want to false accuse an innocent person but on that day he saw someone, a man he knew slightly, parking a car near his. But he thinks that person went down the same footpath. You see he wasn't paying any attention because our dog was playing up and trying to fight another one and that was all he could think of.'

'All the same,' said Dave. 'You must report this to the police and then they will eliminate this other person. They won't make false accusations they just want to narrow down their search field.'

'All right,' she sounded subdued. 'I'll tell my husband to go to the police.'

Josie came back into the room. 'This came addressed to you, special delivery. I had to sign for it.'

'Who knows my address here?'

Josie grinned. 'I should think the whole world does. You put it on the website remember.'

The letter was what is generally called a jiffy bag. Dave opened it and out dropped a CD disk. With it was a brief note. *These are the yacht club CCTV tapes you asked for. We've put them on disk and edited them for the bits you wanted. Cheers for now. Colin.*

Dave almost leapt at his computer and slipped in the disk. 'Oh, Jesus, girl, come look at this.'

'That's Ollavasen,' Josie caught her breath, 'But, that girl in the background I think I know her, or I seem to have met her somewhere. If only the picture was clearer.'

'Yes, I know her name, but I've only met her that once, but that was in a pub in Plymouth just before Trans-Atlantic race. More recently I've seen her picture, but I could be wrong, and look at the bloke with her; no doubt who he is, and that motor, the picture's blurred but I would know that one anywhere.' He looked at her with a broad grin. 'Do I pass this on to the police?'

'I don't know,' she replied. 'Do you consider it that significant?'

'It could be, but what's on here all happened weeks before Ollavasen was killed.'


'That's it,' said Emily. 'She pointed at an odd looking box next to the office telephone. 'That's the panic alarm. The police say I've got to have it.'

'I must say,' said Tom. 'I'm much happier to know you've got it.'

'They tell me Smidgin is out but the prison authorities had long talk with him and it's odd. I don't quite get it.'

'Don't get what?'

'They say that in jail Smidgin has become very repentant and had some sort of religious conversion and he wants reconciliation. He can't have that with his ex-wife and her partner because they've moved to Spain, so he wants to talk to me.'

'Don't buy it. It's a trick.'

'I shall be very careful if he turns up here, but I will listen and I've always got that,' she pointed at the emergency phone.

'All right, but keep your alarm button handy and don't let him in the house. Keep the door chains on at all times. Anyway I'm going to be working from home the next few days.'

'I've different news,' said Emily. 'Dave's girl, Josie rang. They're both off to Australia for the Banner, all expenses paid.'

'What's all that about?'

'Tracing Crickerman to his roots.'

'Good luck to them and,' he laughed. 'It's winter down there.'

Tom walked across to where Peter was sitting in his buggy. Tom pulled a face and the little man gurgled with pleasure. Emily wondered if they really deserved this happiness. The world was full of troubles and some of them were intruding into her peaceful world. Next Thursday she had been briefed to do another prosecution. This time a violent man had repeatedly broken an exclusion order and threatened his ex-girl friend. Yes, she was lucky in her life but maybe too lucky. She glanced out of the window trying to remember what Smidgin looked like two years ago. If he did turn up at the house would she know him?

'Hey, Tom, we haven't eaten out properly since Peter was born. Dave rang earlier and I suggested we all went for a curry this evening. He can't do it because he's stuck in London. How about it?'

'Lily's coming in isn't she?'

'Yeah she'll keep an eye on the boy while she watches telly and we can have a good nosh in the Broad Street curry house.'

Dave never ceased to be amazed by the blasé attitude of the Banner's chief crime correspondent. 'Give me the number of the motor and I'll get the owner for you – no worries,' he told Dave.

'But that's only available on the police central computer or the licensing people.'

'Don't worry about it, Dave. We have our ways. Go off and have a bite to eat and come back at two o'clock.'

Dave took the man's advice and strolled down to a fast food joint near the Banner office block. The fatty burgers were not really his favourite, but would do for now until he got home. The previous evening he had extracted the number of the black Volvo from the Plymouth CCTV footage. Yes, it was the same car, the one with the dented door that he had seen outside Mulberry Lane Charters in Hamble. But it could belong to any one of four persons and he needed to confirm the identity of the girl with Ed Coulden in the CCTV footage. He had seen her just once before briefly in Plymouth and then seen her photo.

It was a warm morning and Dave was able to carry his food out and sit at a pavement table. Here he took out his mobile phone and rang the offices of a top yachting magazine.

'I understand that Hengist Crickerman has a Yacht in Australia and that he came fourth in the Sydney-Hobart. Thanks, this is my number for you to ring back.'

Dave smiled. His intuition was working overtime. This magazine owed him a favour and he hoped they would come good with the information he needed.

His mobile was ringing; it was the magazine. 'Thanks, confirm that the yacht's name is *Sea Eagle*. Thanks, and they must have published a crew list. Can you find that for me and email it.'

Dave finished his meal at leisure. He could afford to; he was already feeling rather pleased with himself. He returned to the Banner offices and the crime reporter was waiting for him. 'Got the name of the Volvo's owner. It's this one: jet black fairly old 1997 model and the owner is one Samantha Christina Halderholm.'

'That follows,' said Dave. 'I only saw her once in Plymouth and in a picture in her brother's office. Interesting thing from our point of view is that both the brother and she had good cause to hate Olla-vasen.'

'Hey, Dave, I've picked up something much more juicy.'

'Tell me more.'

'That bloke Evans that found the Le Bois girl's body. He edits a mag called Surrey Today, right?'

'Yes I've heard that.'

'My local contact in Guildford tells me that Michelle Le Bois submitted an article about the Branham Lake abduction and that little girl Emily…'

'All right, I can guess. It was malignant crap and he rejected it.'

'More than that. Le Bois assaulted him and smashed his office computer.'

'I'm not surprised,' said Dave. 'The woman had an obsession about her uncle being killed by the SAS. But the man had lost it, was insane. He tried to grab Emily as she ran from the fire. There was nothing else they could do.'

'Could Evans have a motive for murder?'

'Nothing I can find about him suggests that and don't we agree there's no connection with Ollavasen.'

'Can you probe a bit on this one, Dave?'

'All right, Harry. I will see if I can find out more.'

Dave had finished for that day, so he drove home to Bayswater. Josie was out and all was quiet. He picked up the phone and dialled the Stoneman's number. Emily answered. 'Hi, Dave. I thought me and Tom might go out for a curry this evening – you want to come?'

'Sorry, can't this time. I'm stuck in London. Look can you tell me anything about Edwin Coulden's sister?'

'Yes, I know them both. Ed used to work for my Dad but they didn't get on or rather Ed wound up the other guys in the sail loft.'

That fitted with the rumours Dave had picked up already. Coulden was said to have something of a persecution complex and hadn't lasted in any job that long.

Emily continued. 'His sister is Nicola and she's all right, she's the one we met working in the pub at Itchenor. I used to go to school with her in Chichester years ago. She was the bright one – got A grades.'

'Do you know if either have been in Australia in recent years?'

'Oh yes, Nicky was full of it. You see Ed was crewing for Crickerman out there as well, but something happened. I don't think it was anything to do with sailing but something Crickerman said or did really wound up Nicky and she wouldn't talk about it.'

'But, Emily. This Nicky Coulden, you say she's the one we all met at Itchenor, yes?

'That's right, but I haven't seen her for a year or two.'

'This is important. Nicky mentioned that her boyfriend skippered boats for Mulberry Lane Charters.'

'That's right. Jason Senessen, he's another half-Danish bloke. Nicky's been shacked up with him for years.'

'Good, that's a name I've been given of someone with a grievance against Alfred Ollavasen.'

'How come, Dave?'

'Peter Jurgen my Danish contact, rang me this afternoon he says Senessen was suspected of nobbling a racing sail in Denmark. Nothing was proved, but hear this. It was Ollavasen that accused him.'

'I met Jason a couple of times,' said Emily. 'He's a good looker and sexy. Not as good looking as present company. He always seemed a bit miserable though.'

'What about the sexy bit?' Dave heard Tom's banter.

'Nicky's never complained, but as for you husband dear?' he heard Emily laugh. 'You're not bad either.'


Walter Smidgin was free and he still felt insecure. Prison had provided a sort of security and a routine that he understood. Now he was released and in the world again, so what now? His wife was long gone and his house in Hamble sold to pay debts. He no longer had a business and no one in the world of boats would trust him again. Yes, he had been a fucking idiot. The psychiatrists had told him he was something called a control freak. He had had sessions on anger-management, but his time with the chaplain had been different. He had a different focus on life now and maybe he would find solace in the work with offenders towards which he had been pointed.

Walter couldn't return to Hamble but his sister had offered him shelter in her pub and B&B. He liked this place. It was a popular venue for wedding receptions and celebrations and Walter had always liked the atmosphere of the place. More important there was a good chance no one would have any idea who he was. Once settled there he could send out his first olive branch to that little barrister who had sent him down. For weeks he had hated her and planned his retribution.

Then he had thought again. He had been his own worst enemy. How did he think he could get away with his plot? The barrister had only done her job.

Botley wasn't the easiest place to reach from this part of Sussex but he had a travel voucher and enough pocket money to get by. A mixture of travel by bus and train took him to his destination in late afternoon. Sandra, his sister, had loyally visited him in nick and gave him a welcome with no recriminations.

'I'll show you your room,' she said. 'We're a bit busy this evening. We've a celebration party and you may want to keep out of the way.'

'Why, it's not an old lags gathering?'

She laughed. 'It's a lot of yachting folk. It's a reunion of the winning crew in the double trans-Atlantic race a few months back.'

Walter shook his head. 'Don't know any of them. I met their skipper once, Crickerman, but I've heard he's in the shit too with the law.'

'What did you think of him?'

'No comment.'

Walter dropped his tiny travel bag on the bed then he took a shower. Prison stank and it was a relief to wash away the last traces of that stink real or imaginary. He had only the one set of ordinary civilian clothes and he would need to extend this wardrobe before he went for his job interview. Having showered shaved and dressed he found his way down to the main bar. It was a nice happy scene and crowded with the celebrating yachties. He didn't recognise any of them which was something of a relief. Sandra served him with a pint.

She held up a hand to her eyes. 'Sun's very low in the sky and it's blazing through that window. Could you pull the curtains?'

Walter walked across the lounge and gave a pull on the curtains. Nothing happened so he gave a harder jerk and the whole thing came away in his hands including a long heavy old fashioned curtain rail with an ugly sharp point on each end.

'Sorry,' he called. 'My fault.'

'Don't worry dear. That curtain rail is supposed to be an antique but health and safety were on about it being dangerous. I'll get the whole lot replaced next week.'

At that moment one of the crewmen walked through the bar door carrying his full glass and Walter knew him. He couldn't off hand remember the guy's name but he was a Hamble pro-yachtsman whom Walter had crossed in the past and the man had reputation for short-fused temper. Even as Walter turned away the man tripped on the fallen curtain rod nearly slurping his glass full over the floor.

The crowd in the bar laughed 'Watch it, Ed,' someone shouted. 'Pissed already?'

'I'll get rid of this bloody thing,' the man replied, picking up the curtain rod and projecting it, javelin fashion, through the open window.

'Hi, cool it, Ed, darling – that temper of yours. This is a party for God's sake.'

The man turned round. He had a lopsided grin. 'Sorry, Nicky.'

The whole room had suddenly gone quiet. The revellers by the bar were staring toward the door and there stood two uniformed police officers, one male one female. Neither had removed their caps and neither looked as it they were here for pleasure.

'Mr Walter Smidgin?' said the male officer. Walter remembered this man for his enforced stay in Winchester police station. Suddenly he felt his old rage returning.

'What's it to you?' he snarled.

'May we talk to you in private?'

Walter took a pace forward. 'You can bloody say anything you want to here. I've only just got out of prison and I haven't done a thing.'

'Very well,' said the officer. 'It's what you're planning to do that concerns us and if I've witnesses to this warning maybe that's a good thing.'

'What fucking warning?'

'There's a young woman near Alresford: Mrs Emily Stoneman. You've got a grievance and you've threatened to hurt her. Don't argue it was reported in prison.'

Despite everything Walter felt the red mist build as of old. 'That crafty bitch put me away. I owe her and you won't stop me – bastards.'

'Mr Smidgin, that sort of talk won't do. Keep away from the lady. You've been formally warned.' The two officers left. Suddenly the room had become silent.

'Why are you fucking lot staring?' Walter shouted. He turned on his heel and walked out into the fresh air. The police car was just leaving the car park.

Walter took a deep breath and forced himself to calm down. He had had a serious lapse of his new discipline. He thought about going back inside but that would mean a ticking off from Sandra and more embarrassment. Instead he turned and decided to walk off his rage.

Emily and Tom were eating breakfast when the front door bell rang accompanied by a heavy knocking.

'I'll go,' said Tom.

He had a shock. Standing there was a suited man he didn't know and two police officers.

'I am Chief Inspector Marchway of Hampshire Police and I would like to ask you some questions.' The tone was unfriendly.

'Hello, Inspector,' said Emily who had appeared behind Tom.

'Good morning Mrs Stoneman, may we come in please?'

'Of course you can,' she smiled. 'How can we help?'

All three policemen were now in the house. The Inspector had an attitude cold and unfriendly and for some reason the uniformed constables were walking around staring at the cottage windows.

'Mr and Mrs Stoneman, would you care to tell me where you were between six o'clock and nine thirty yesterday evening?'

'We weren't robbing a bank if that's what you think,' said Tom.

'Shut up, Tom,' Emily snapped. 'Inspector, why do you want to know?'

'There has been an incident. Because of that incident we require you both to state your movements on the day and times I've stated.'

Emily sighed audibly. 'All right have it your own way. At six o'clock we were here in this house. If you ask our nanny, Mrs Lorrimer, she will confirm that. At six forty five we left the house and drove to Alresford and parked in Broad Street. At seven we took up our pre-booked table at the curry house. We know the staff well and they will confirm it. We paid our bill at exactly ten o'clock, wait a minute,' she paused and rummaged in her handbag. 'I've still got the receipt somewhere, yes here it is,' she held up a slip of paper. 'We left the premises and drove reaching home at ten fifteen as Mrs Lorrimer will confirm.'

'God deliver me from barristers,' Grunted Marchway.

'Sir, called one of the constables. 'All these windows are too small and the curtains are in place.'

'No more than I expected. I think the answer to that is in the Tenetbury Arms.'

'The pub at Botley?' Tom was even more puzzled now. 'Can you tell us what's happened?'

'I'm sure your story will check out,' said Marchway. 'I'm sorry if we've upset you but there's been another murder incident and it concerns you.'

'Oh, come on Inspector,' said Emily. 'You must tell us. If it concerns either Tom or me we've a right to know.'

'An ex-prisoner, Walter Smidgin was stabbed in woods near Curbridge.'

'Oh, God, it just gets worse,' Emily began to sob and Tom put his arms around her.

'Is he dead?' asked Tom.

'Yes, he's dead.'

'He threatened me,' Emily gasped. 'But I'd never wanted him dead.'

'I know,' said Marchway. He was friendly and relaxed now. 'We had to check you, but I've no doubt he had enemies. A man like that always does.'

# CHAPTER 22

'Hi, Kiwi Dave, had any sheep lately?'

Dave laughed. 'No, not sheep, your great-great how many times granddad stole them all before they sent him here.'

They were certainly in a different world now, thought Josie. The barman had not been intentionally offensive, she could see that. No doubt he was giving what to him was a cheerful greeting. Dave was totally unfazed and simply grinned. This was a different world and Josie was rather enjoying it. Certainly in a sailing club in England the reception would have been cheerful, yes; but with a polite leavening.

They had arrived in Melbourne six hours earlier. Somehow the Banner had pulled strings and they had their entry visas waiting at Heathrow. The nearly twenty four hour flight had been a grind as would be the flight in the autumn to Auckland and their wedding. That would be a joyful moment in both their lives, but now this was business.

They had a hire car and a guide, a reporter from a local radio station. This girl had been polite and helpful and had seen them settled in their hotel in Collins Street. From there they had driven to a sailing club where Dave had been a member. Although this was southern hemisphere winter Josie was warm enough in the watery sunlight and blue sky. This was not the gloom and doom of January in Southern England. But the city itself was impressive: clean with tall buildings and no visible signs of poverty and recession, but then they hadn't seen the seedier side.

'Naah, mate, not sheep,' said Dave. 'This one's better,' his voice dropped to a whisper. 'She's a Pom though.'

'Well, maybe, but they can't help it,' the barman guffawed.

Josie was too tired to be offended as they carried their drinks to a table. 'Sorry about the back chat,' said Dave. 'Bit of a culture shock, but this is Oz – uncouth lot.'

'How did he know you come from New Zealand? You all sound the same.'

'Not to the practised ear we don't. Look, everyone in the UK speaks English but put a Scotsman in Devon and then you'll notice him. It's the same here. They see us Kiwis as country bumpkins; we reckon them as criminals made good, but it's all in best humour; or is until the All Blacks pound them to bits.'

'They call us Poms,'

'Yes, supposed to be because the early settlers arrived with red cheeks like pomegranates. Ignore the jibes. Give'em back as good as you get. We all throw these insults at each other, but it's for fun; basically it's because we're all family even if we never admit it.' Dave leaned across and stroked her hand affectionately.

'That barman seemed to know you?'

'Yeah, Matt. I've sailed from this club quite a few times. That guy's been here for years.'

Dave's mobile phone shrilled and he pulled it out of his jacket pocket. 'Yes, I'm David Manning. Yes, I can do that. I'd be so pleased to meet you. I've my fiancé with me. May she come as well? Thank you Mrs Crickerman, if you can give me directions we'll be right over.'

Dave put down his mobile and grinned broadly. 'Wow, that's Crickerman's ex-missus she's dead keen to talk to me about something.'

'How did she know that you were here?'

'I didn't expect her to be interested but the Banner's sister paper, awful sheet, said they would contact her.' He stood up. 'Come on, girl let's be going.'


'No prints on the murder weapon and precious little else to go on,' said Inspector Marchway.

'Could this be any connection with our other two murders?' asked Superintendent Hollins.

'I can't see how it can. Ollavasen and Le Bois looked premeditated but this one is much more an impulse killing. Smidgin was a man who made enemies. He was probably safer in prison than out. I guess someone recognised him in that pub and decided to fix him using that lethal curtain rod. That was never premeditated.'

'I take it all the people in that place have been questioned?'

'Yes, sir. A few locals never left the place throughout and the others were a party of yacht crew celebrating.'

Hollins was clearly not satisfied. 'Can they all be accounted for all the time? Smidgin worked around the yacht scene at Hamble. Someone in that party may have had a motive.'

'I know that, sir. But the yacht is based in Lymington and only one of her crew has connections with Hamble. Most admit to having sailed there once but that's it. Only this one Edwin Coulden actually lives and works there.'

'Were any of them seen to leave the room during the likely murder time?'

'That's where it gets difficult. Seems they were in and out of the bar all evening. Off to the toilet and then out to use their phones or to smoke. We've taken all the contacts from them but frankly, sir, they seemed pretty genuine to me.'

'I gather our two officers interviewed Smidgin and he reverted to type.'

'Oh yes, sir. All that stuff they gave him in jail. You know anger management, spiritual experiences; makes you sick.'

'Did our officers notice anything?'

'Only that Smidgin wouldn't talk in private. Started blustering in front of everyone. Then our men saw him standing outside the pub as they drove off.'

Hollins sat back in his chair. 'No, Smidgin's enemy was in that pub and he took an impulse decision. Could have been somebody standing in the doorway. The murder weapon was there in easy reach. No this was a spur of the moment job.'

'The way he stormed out, sir. Had he decided to go to Alresford and confront Mrs Stoneman?'

'From Botley to Alresford is a good long walk and there's no cars missing.'

Marchway paused. He had his own theories but they might not impress his chief. 'Sir I think it's worth recording that the yacht crew celebration was for winning the two leg Trans Atlantic race. The yacht belongs to Hengist Crickerman although he couldn't be there for obvious reasons. That does give us a tenuous link to Ollavasen.'

'But that's not going to help us with this one. I don't suppose Smidgin ever met Ollavasen.'

'There's one more coincidence, sir, if it is a coincidence. There's a ramblers hostel a few doors away from the pub and there was a group staying there at the time and that group was led by the man Evans, the same as was at Greatswood, and reported the Le Bois murder.'

'That's certainly interesting. What was Mr Evans doing at the time?'

'We're not sure, sir, but there's no proof that he went anywhere near the pub or saw Smidgin.'

Hollins groaned. 'Oh for a quiet life. We're going to get a roasting from the tabloids.'

'Something else, sir, concerning Evans. Surrey Police have passed me a report. We know Evans employed Michelle Le Bois freelance. He never told us that he called the police when she vandalised his office.'

'Let's go,' Dave gave a whoop. 'This is breakthrough.'

'Where exactly are we going?' Josie sounded less than enthused.

'I've set it in the satnav, but it's some sort of mansion out Healesville way.'

They drove out of the city. Dave hardly noticed the countryside, of vineyards and rolling hills. He was rehearsing his notes and the questions he wanted answered. He was more than ever certain that the solution to this puzzle must lie in Australia. That chance remark he had overheard still jarred. It didn't make sense. They were now driving through a landscape that could have been Surrey in the UK apart from the post boxes at the entrance of every gravel drive.

*'You have arrived at your destination.'* The satnav announced.

'She sounds like Chloe,' Josie giggled.

'This is it,' Dave stared at the sign board. *'Cool Yarra Court.* Does she mean cool in temperature or cool in teenspeak. Can't be that she's well over fifty. And we're miles from the Yarra, can't even see it from anywhere around here.'

He pulled up in front of a pair of formidable looking gates. 'This is like that Greatswood Manor; very un-Australian.' He climbed out and went through the familiar ritual with the gate telephone. 'Ok, mate, welcome to Cool Yarra. I'll open the gates and you can come on up.' The voice was female and definitely Australian.

The gates swung open as Dave climbed back in the car. 'Reckon that was the good lady herself I spoke to. At least no poncy butler this time.'

'What do we know about this woman?' asked Josie.

'She married Crickerman when she was nineteen. Her parents ran small chain of grocery stores. Crickerman turned them into a global empire. As you might expect the marriage never lasted. Crickerman put it around too much with the girls so she divorced him and the only son's a rich hippy in California.'

The last turn in the approach drive revealed the house: a large bungalow structure, painted white with multiple extensions. Even in mid winter the gardens were neat and trim and surrounded by exotic tropical shrubs. A shiny Honda four by four stood parked by the front entrance.

'Come on, Josie. Let's see what the lady is like.'

Josie giggled. 'I bet she's another Dame Edna.'

'Hiya, you must be David,' a shrill voice called.

Both of them turned to see a petite figured fair-haired woman dressed in jeans and a red fleece top. She had leather knee pads strapped on and carried a garden trug.

'Hi, I'm Donna. Glad to meet you. Let's go indoors and have a drink.'

Dave and Josie's eyes met and Josie grinned back. He knew neither of them had expected a reception like this.

'Scuse' the state I'm in,' said Donna. 'Been sorting out me vegi patch. Gotta' do better this year – bad drought last summer. You Kiwis've got the climate we've got the sunshine and too much most years.'

She pointed them across a hallway and into a well furnished lounge and invited them to sit. 'What'll you drink? I reckon a glass of Shiraz from my own vineyard.'

'Just one for me,' said Dave. 'I'm driving.'

'Yeah, sure – the local dicks are getting hot on that.'

She poured the drinks and Dave took a sip. The wine was good: a nice fragrance and a good robust taste on the pallet.

'Right, folks. I'm Donna Crickerman. I know that my ex is in the shit but he never killed that girl. Heng is all mouth and trousers but I doubt he'd kill a mouse.'

'I must say I've been coming round to that view myself,' said Dave. 'It's very complicated and now we've had three murders and they may be linked.'

'Yeah,' said Donna. 'I had this call from Bogger Roger at Radio…'

'Who?'

'Roger Ralaglio, he's a shock jock. Bloody rude normally even by our Aussie standards. He's a bastard, but I like him. He said you were a decent guy and you might help dig Hengist out of the shit if I answered your questions.'

So that was it. Dave remembered that the Banner's proprietor had local radio franchises in Australia.

'Right, let's have your questions – fire away.'

'Mrs Crickerman…'Dave began.

'Oh for Chrissake. You've been picking up Pom ways. Look, I'm Donna and you're Dave – Ok?'

'Er, Donna, sorry to be blunt, but was the murdered girl Dione Logan one of your problems?'

'She may have been but there were a dozen others – the man was insatiable. As for this Dione I'd never heard of her before I was told she was murdered. Sorry about that of course.'

'Can you think of anyone who might hate your ex-husband enough to stitch him up for murder?'

'Not really. He had business rivals of course, but it wasn't like that. Might be one of the girls of course but I don't know a thing about his UK floosies. Bet there were plenty.'

Dave nodded and wrote a note on his pad. 'You know there was a problem over a yacht race?'

'Oh yeah, the idiot tried to buy an easy win: bound to cause trouble. That was his ego of course.' Donna walked across the lounge and poured another glass of wine.

'I'm afraid I've got to ask this,' said Dave. 'But was there any special incident that really was the last straw between you?'

'Oh, my God yes. That little girl might be vengeful and she was a Brit.'

Dave looked questioningly at her.

'Three years ago Heng brought his boat back to Melbourne after the Sydney Hobart race. By the by, I like sailing but he would never let me on his boat – I wonder why?' She laughed but there was no humour in the sound. 'He wasn't happy, that's probably why he wasn't careful. You see on the last stretch of the race up the Derwent River to Hobart our boat *Sea Eagle* was leading. Then Heng has an ego attack. He takes over the helm and hits something or sticks on some shallows, not sure which and two others pass him to the finish. Cripes was he hopping mad about it. He was still third in class on corrected time and fourth overall, but it was his own fault – silly sod.'

'I can sympathise,' said Dave. 'I've done a Sydney Hobart once myself – but we'd have celebrated for a month if we'd managed fourth.'

'The trouble was the way he worked off his frustrating. He took this little Brit girl and he made her preggers. He never took precautions like he did with all the others. Then the hassle starts.' Donna's expression had changed. She looked upset.

'I said let the girl have the kiddy and we'd adopt it. She wanted to keep it anyway. But then Heng barges in and says no it's gotta' be an abortion.'

'What happened then?' Josie had intervened.

'Heng drugged the poor little thing. Then he drove her to the clinic and lashed out the dollar bills. But the abort was forced and that was the final straw for me. I told him he'd inherited some of his old man's

Nazi manners. I divorced the bastard and I did Ok financially. Plenty of cash and I've got the marital home here – not that he was ever in it much.'

'Can you give me a name for this girl?'

'No, sorry, I was that disgusted I kept out of it. But she had a close friend, another UK girl called Nicky and she had a brother who crewed on Heng's boat.

'Sorry to interrupt,' said Dave, 'but do you remember the brother's name?'

'Yes, I do, sort of – he was…he was Ed, I remember that because he was a lahdidah plum-mouthed Pom; signed his name as Edwin for god's sake. Heng said he was a bolshie sod.'

'Did this Nicola have her boyfriend with her?'

'Yeah, she did. Good looker he was but a bit miserable – never said much.'

'Was he called Jason?'

'Dunno, never heard his other name, but as I remember Heng's Floosie was pretty down, but this Nicky was bloody angry; threatened Heng to his face. I never asked questions but they'll know at the big noise yacht club. That's where they all gathered.'

'I know it,' said Dave.

'They couldn't expel Heng because of the girl; he was too rich to touch.' She paused and glanced at an antique long-case clock. 'Here, it's twelve thirty; how about a bite to eat – is it lunch you call it in the UK?'

'That'll be nice, eh Josie?' said Dave.

Josie smiled happily.

'It's not Barbecue weather,' said Donna, 'but we'll do our best.'

The lunch had proved an understatement in Josie's view. It was in fact a tribute to Australian hospitality. Josie had wondered how Donna managed this huge house on her own. In the end a cook house keeper appeared assisted by a teenage girl who had of course to be named Kylie. It was a total contrast to Dave's description of Greatswood Manor. No butler and no deference whatever. The staff sat down to eat with the guests. The fare was almost overwhelming: huge steaks and piles of vegetables and salads washed down with more Shiraz.

'Come back at Christmas,' said Donna, 'and we'll have the pool filled for a swim.'

'Thanks, but we'll be in NZ then. We two are tying the knot and you'd be very welcome.'

'Oh, that's great. I'd love that.'

Now they were on the road again heading back into the city. 'Where next?' Josie asked.

'We're off to Port Philip and the poshest Yacht club you'll find anywhere south of Cowes.' He loosed a gale of laughter.

'You mean a different one from this morning?' asked Josie.

'Too right, this one's still stuck with Pom ways. Think of it we're in Oz and they've got a dress code. You can't wear thongs in the club house.'

Josie gaped at him. 'I'm wearing ordinary knickers as you know and I'm not dropping my trousers for inspection.'

'Oh no, girl. I didn't mean undies. It's a definition clash. Thongs are slip on summer sandals, what you lot call flippy-flops. The old farts are allergic to bare toes, even though yours are quite pretty.'

'That's a relief and even here it's not that warm anyway.'

'I thought we might wind up at this place so I came prepared,' Dave laughed again. 'I think I'd better wear this. He dangled a neck tie in her face. Can't remember when I last put on one of these.'

They arrived at the yacht club and parked the car. Josie was impressed with the beautiful expanse of water that was St Kilda Bay. Her apprehension was soon lost when they entered the clubhouse and met the secretary. 'Mr Manning, welcome, we all enjoyed your articles on the Olifa Olympics last year. Your girl won gold as well.'

'Chloe? Yes, but she's a naturalised Brit now and in their army,'

'Yes, we're aware of that as well. She won a medal in Afghanistan I believe.'

'That's right.'

The man's mood changed. 'Mr Manning, I gather you've not come to talk about the Olympics. Am I right that your visit concerns the conduct of one of our members?'

'Yes, you can say that.'

'Mr Manning, please come into my office and your young lady as well.'

Dave was intrigued. This man had a leavening of Aussie speech but he must once have been a Pom. Well no disgrace in that. Tens of thousands of Brits had made good in Australia however quickly the whingers had fled home.

'Please be seated,' the secretary waved them to a comfortable leather sofa. 'Now regarding the man Crickerman we have seriously considered expelling this person for conduct likely to bring us into disrepute. But we feel we must wait until the resolution of his present troubles. For some reason that man is popular in this country and especially in this city.'

'I won't sit in judgement about this London crime,' said Dave. 'As I said on the phone to you it's his conduct with the young girl three years ago. You see I suspect she may have an influence on the happenings in London.'

'Hmm,' the secretary was deep in thought. 'The poor little girl would have good reason to hate him, but on the contrary she seems to have been infatuated with that man. Maybe she had eyes on his fortune after our Donna divorced him.'

'Donna Crickerman – you know her?' Dave was surprised.

'She's a cousin of my own good wife,' the secretary replied.

Dave was pleased. So here was a Brit who had made the journey to the other side of the earth, married a local girl and made good. 'Do you know anything about the London girl the one who was murdered?'

'Only what the press here have unearthed. She was a local girl born in Werribee somewhere near the zoo. Her father worked there. University graduate worked for Qualistores in the city here and followed Crickerman to England. Obviously that was a bad move. The popular media say she was also infatuated with the man.' He paused. 'Mr Manning, I must say that even though we had reservations about Mr Crickerman, we never saw anything of a violent tendency. Highly duplicitous, yes, but a murderer never.'

Dave thought carefully about this next question. 'What can you tell me about the British girl that Crickerman got into trouble?'

'Actually we had two British girls there that month. I'll check their names for you on our register of temporary members. But the one Crickerman abused, she was a pretty girl. Sang nicely at one of our socials. She had been working in Sydney with this friend of hers and they appeared here about the time Crickerman brought his boat *Sea Eagle* for haul out. From everything we heard she appears to have been deeply in love with the fellow.' The secretary slid the computer mouse around, clicked it and then pressed the print button. 'Here you are; these are the ladies.' He ringed two names on a list and handed the paper slip to Dave. The club secretary looked around and dropped his voice. 'Something happened at our post race celebration. I think you should know that the abused girl was very depressed and silent, but her friend was vocal. Worse still she had a young man, I think he was Danish or similar: name of Senessen; a very rude aggressive fellow. We had to warn him about his conduct.'

'What did he do?' asked Josie.

'I tell you this. They both confronted Crickerman in the entry hall here and threatened to kill him.'

Dave read the two girls names and was not entirely surprised, but this proved nothing. He would follow the trail when they got back home. Home! What the hell was he thinking? His home was Auckland not Bayswater. What would his dad say if he thought his son was turning Pom?

# CHAPTER 23

Hengist Crickerman's mood varied between rage and despair. Why couldn't those stupid police understand that he'd never killed anyone ever? He'd never arranged for anyone to be killed. Yes, he'd cut a few legal corners in building his business but it had never occurred to him to kill anyone. Dione was a silly girl. Why had he brought her with him to London? Yes, all right the girl was intelligent and quick witted and had lots of skill in bed. But she was jealous and couldn't accept the other girls. She'd threatened Marie and Laura and even his little navigator, Susanna, but hell; that one was a bloody lessie dike and tied up with that fat Kiwi bitch; no wouldn't be her. So, who had killed Dione? For that matter who had killed that Danish slob Ollavasen? He hadn't ordered any killing but it could have been the Le Bois girl. She had the details, the passwords and numbers of the offshore account. Yes, she could have killed Ollavasen and kept the money. What was more she had refused to bed with himself; refused him, for God's sake. Weedy white-faced little bimbo, how could she refuse such a gift? Who did she think she was?

But she couldn't have killed Dione in a fit of jealousy because she was dead already. So who killed Le Bois and Dione? Who was the most jealous of his lovers? Janet could have done it, or Tracy or that Scottish bit of skirt Brenda. What about that Nicky in Oz; she'd threatened to kill him. Said it to his face and at the time he reckoned she meant it. He sank into a chair and put his head in his hands and once again raged at the sight of the stupid police tag locked around his right ankle. Oh, hell, would none of these Poms believe him? There could be another death if they tried to put him in jail. Yes, he would kill himself.

The telephone was ringing, the landline one in the office. He would answer it but he'd better be careful, the police would be monitoring it. How did they expect him to keep both hands on a multi billion dollar business if he couldn't speak frankly to his minions?

'Hello,' he carried the phone back into the lounge. 'Oh hello, I'd been thinking about you're offer if I can call it that. Yes. But I can't speak on this line and you can't come here. I'm off limits.' He listened in increasing irritation. 'No, you're wasting your time and mine. Shove off!' he slammed the phone back on its mount. For the first time since childhood he was suffocating in a fog of misery.

'It looks as it the Le Bois woman was on the fiddle,' Inspector Marchway addressed his crime team. This had been augmented by two more detectives seconded to him since the Smidgin killing. 'The figures tattooed on her arm are not in fact tattoos only normal indelible ink. I must give credit to our Scotland Yard friends who have turned very heavy with the banking system and extracted confidential information.' He looked around and wished his men would show a little bit more enthusiasm. 'Yes, half a million US dollars salted away in an offshore account in the Cayman Islands and the figures were the account numbers and passwords. So we have an additional motive for the murder and a pretty good one.'

'Do we know the origin of this money?' asked the woman sergeant.

'Good question but the answer is no. We're not meant to make guesses, but it just could be the money that was due to Ollavasen for throwing that yacht race.'

He checked his notes. 'We're no further forward in the Smidgin killing despite an intense search of the wood where the body was found. The victim was stabbed with the steel curtain rail with an ornamental spear point, and there were no signs that he made any resistance. Could this victim also have known his killer? This is a remote area although we have made a door to door check. There are few houses there and no one saw anything unusual.' The fact was he had to tell his team they were getting nowhere very slowly.

'Sir,' called the same sergeant. 'I gather uniform have talked to everyone in the hotel and not all the movements have been confirmed.'

'That is so, but the jolly sailors were for ever pissing in the toilets or slipping out to smoke. None of them were all in the room at the same time. Two things: physically any of them could have wielded that spear. They are all strong muscular types and our surgeon says the spear was driven in with force. But it is still the case; who among that lot had the slightest motive to kill Smidgin? No, it must have been someone with a very good reason.'

'Sir, could the enemy be an inmate of the prison?'

Marchway nodded. 'Yes, that's good thinking and we are checking all prisoners released from Ford in the last month and, if needed, we can go back further. However I feel this could have a background in sailing and for that reason I think I will visit the Stoneman family again. I need to clear the air anyway as I was a bit too heavy with them on my last visit.'

This time Marchway phoned in advance and made an appointment. Emily Stoneman was at home and seemed to be having some hassle with a fractious baby. She was friendly and agreed for him to visit at six that evening when both she and her husband would be home. Marchway wasn't sure that this couple could be much help, but he knew Emily to be one of the sharpest young barristers on the circuit and she might have remembered something.

'Come on in, Inspector,' said Emily. She waved him into their sitting room where her husband Tom was watching television. The growing baby was bouncing and dangling in a walking harness and making guggling noises. Tom looked up smiled and turned off the TV.

'How can we help?' Emily asked.

'It's the dead man Smidgin. You crossed him and we all know why, but can you name any others in Hamble or around the sailing scene who might have a quarrel with him?'

Emily's face registered surprise. 'He was a rude abrasive character but I doubt anyone wanted him dead.'

'No, Mrs Stoneman, somebody did. We think somebody in that pub that day recognised him and took the chance of retribution.'

'Was there any similarity with the other murders?'

Marchway shook his head. 'No real similarities. The Ollavasen and Le Bois murders were performed with a sharpened blade. In our opinion both were premeditated. The Smidgin killing was performed with an antique curtain rail which happened to have very sharp end points. Smidgin didn't attempt to defend himself so he may have known the assailant. But I can tell you it was an angry assault by someone with a strong arm.'

Tom Stoneman looked up. He hesitated before he spoke. 'I do have one suggestion but maybe I'm a bit biased.'

'No please tell me.'

'I understand that the pub was crowded with the sailing fraternity, am I right?' Tom paused.

'Yes that is exactly right.'

'I'm only guessing but did Smidgin shout that he was out to get Emily?'

'Yes, Mr Stoneman that is most perceptive, but indeed he screamed and blustered about it. He sounded vicious. Our officers noted this and all our witnesses confirm it.'

'Emily here is a big name in sailing and she's also very popular, I would say loved in the broadest sense.'

Emily cackled in laughter. 'Oh, come off it. Are you saying one of those yachties is jealous of my medal?'

Tom's expression was now wholly serious. 'On the contrary I think someone who likes you took Smidgin's bluster so seriously that he decided to intervene before Smidgin could carry out his intentions. He, the assailant, may not have meant to commit murder but there may have been an argument that got out of hand. I am thinking of some hot blooded character who lost it in the heat of the moment. I can suggest a suspect.' Tom paused and wrote a name.

Marchway was impressed, but wasn't sure. This man was so devoted to his wife that he might be letting his imagination play tricks. 'Mr Stoneman, that is an original suggestion and I have noted it and will take it seriously. Thank you.'

'Wow,' Dave shouted. 'This is more like it.'

'What is?' Josie called from in the shower.

'Email from the Banner editor: says. "Well done David. Keep this up and expect a salary increase."'

Josie emerged from the shower wrapped in a towel and looked at the screen. 'They really like you.'

They had returned through Heathrow sleepy and sweaty and had decided to give themselves the day off.

'Are you going to write something about Australia?' asked Josie.

'Not yet. We've got a lot of information but none of it proves anything. I wish I could talk to Crickerman in person but no chance, while he's on restriction. The only thing I'm now certain of is that he didn't kill anyone. No, this whole tragedy links back to his sex life.'

'Seems he kept a harem.'

'Too right he did and harems I guess are hotbeds of jealousy.'

'His bimbos certainly kept his bed hot.'

Dave's mobile was ringing. 'Hello…' It was Tom Stoneman and he had news to shock even Dave. He put the phone away and turned to Josie. 'There's been another killing.' He explained about the death of Walter Smidgin.

'That's the man Emily sent to jail isn't it?'

'Yes.'

'Can this be anything to do with the other murders?'

'On the face of it no, but Tom thinks it may have been the work of someone who knows Emily.'

'But how come?'

'Because half an hour or so before he was killed Smidgin was boasting he'd get Emily and wait…wait. The point is he screamed it in front of a whole yacht crew and that crew was guess which?'

'I don't know. Tell me.'

'The entire crew of *Qualistores,* minus of course their skipper, were holding a celebration reunion and they were all there when Smidgin made his threats.'

'My God, Dave, that's the most likely motive I would guess. Do we have the names of those at this bash?'

'Oh yes, oh yes – one of them was our mate Ed Coulden and with him was his sister's bloke, Jason Senessen.'

'Would either have a motive?'

'Well, they're both Hamble based sailors and maybe Smidgin got up their noses before. It sound like this was a spontaneous attack and not a planned murder. Maybe the killer only wanted to confront Smidgin and it all went wrong.'

'I've heard that name, Jason whatever before.'

'Yes, in the Melbourne yacht club. He threatened to kill Crickerman. But unless he's a complete psycho he had no real motive to kill Smidgin.'

'But whoever is doing these killings must be psychotic.'

'In that surmise, girl, you are dead right. Excuse the pun. I think I will check out this Jason.'

'Dave, be tactful because his girl is a friend of Emily.'

Dave stood up. 'There's just one more thing I need to do. Have we the phone number of that woman Sophie Evans and her husband? If they give me the name I think they are going to then I'm two jumps in front of the police.'

Ten minutes later he came back into the room looking smug. 'Mrs Evans says two people started off down that footpath before him. They weren't together and started on the path about three minutes apart. The first one was a woman he claims he didn't know, but the second was a guy he's seen around the sailing scene but he wasn't sure of his name. He thought it sounded a bit European. So I asked him was it Senessen. Well, Mrs Evans thought it might be but she would have to ask her husband.'

'But, Dave. Why should this Senessen kill Michelle?'

'Another thought. Why was Evans so keen to point the finger at Senessen? We know Michelle trashed his office.'

'Oh, Dave. This is all a bit too deep for me. Will you tell the police?'

'Yes, of course as soon as I have anything concrete. At the moment they treat me as an idiot reporter. In the meantime I'll check if Mr Senessen is keen on rambling.'

Hengist Crickerman had been subjected to one more session of police questioning. He had followed with great difficulty the advice of his lawyers not to be belligerent and not to bluster at his interrogators. Time and time again he had repeated the truth. His physical relationship with Dione had faded but she was his PA, the best he'd employed and he had absolutely no motive for hurting her. Already he had been through the humiliation of giving DNA samples, the results of which he had not been told.

Now the interrogators had moved on from questioning him about Dione and had switched their target to Michelle Le Bois. Had he met Michelle on the night of Ollavasen's murder. There was now no point in hiding. He admitted his stupidity. Yes, he wanted to win that Atlantic race. He knew that Ollavasen was in desperate straits financially. He'd drunk too much when he first accosted the Dane and suggested he lose the race. Ollavasen appeared to have jumped at the offer. Then after the Plymouth pre-race briefing Ollavasen had tried to back out of the deal. At that point Hengist knew he should have let the idea go but he had been stupid and upped his offer.

What had this got to do with Michelle? Well, the girl was devious and a pest but she was well suited as the go between. He had deposited the money in a Cayman Island bank and taken the precaution of leaving it in the name of Primo Garcia an associate whose fortune had collapsed. Garcia and Michelle were to pay off Ollavasen. Why hadn't Michelle delivered the money to Ollavasen? It was so bloody obvious now. The devious little girl intended to take the money for her own.

He stared at the interrogator. 'So there you are. There's your motive and there's your murderer. Only it didn't do her much good.'

'Inspector Welsh,' said the snooty solicitor. 'You have no case for holding my client. You know you have no case, so what do you intend to do?'

'Very well,' the Inspector looked suitably chastened. 'Mr Crickerman is still a  suspect. However we are prepared to be lenient on bale conditions.'

'I'm pissed off with being in that apartment,' said Hengist. 'Can't I go to my place out of town?'

'Where is that?'

'I've already declared that. It's in Kent – Melbourne House near Sittingbourne.'

'Right,' said Welsh. 'Go there, but you retain the ankle tag and curfew conditions remain.'

Hengists' driver had delivered him back to the apartment and from there he had issued instructions to open up Melbourne House. He hadn't been there since that time a few weeks ago when his stay had been ruined by another pestering nuisance. He hadn't heard a thing since so hopefully he would be left alone to lick his wounds in peace.


'Looks like we've scored one over the MET this time?' Marchways put down the telephone. He knew his face had an ill-concealed smirk. 'They accept that Michelle Le Bois was after the offshore banked money. It looks as if Crickerman is telling the truth. The MET are not happy about that because it's weakening their case when they were so certain they'd hooked a really big fish.'

Hollins agreed, 'However, there's one witness we've not bothered with if he is a witness. There's this South American gentleman staying at Greatswood; Mr or should that be Senor Garcia. It seems he comes from Olifa on the West Coast...

'That's where last year's Olympics were held. It's a small country but by all accounts the games were brilliantly organised,' said Marchway.

'That's true, but it seems this Garcia is not welcome in his own country. His internet betting business failed and the Olifa exchequer have had to pick up the bill. Their justice system is not looking to extradite the man but he's keeping his head down. However it seems most of his debts have been guaranteed by our friend Crickerman and by some twist of fate he's been offered sanctuary at Greatswood by Erich Shilltinberg.'

Marchway was puzzled. 'That's odd, sir. We thought Shilltinberg and Crickerman were on bad terms.'

'Well I've checked the background of both and historically they are polls apart. Crickerman's father was a Nazi who escaped to Australia and Shilltinberg's parents were Jewish refuges in the 1930s. Crickerman junior made himself a billionaire and so did the Shilltinberg's son. Both are or were keen yachtsmen but apart from that I can't see them being friends.'

'Is Garcia still at Greatswood?'

'We've checked and yes he is,' said Hollins. 'I would rather like you to go and have a chat with him.'

'Mrs Wenman and Senor Garcia: Chief Inspector Marchway of Hampshire Constabulary.' The Butler bowed with excessive formality as he showed Marchway into the grand drawing room.

Marchway knew that Mrs Wenman was Erich Shilltinberg's daughter. Standing facing him was the man he had come to see. Garcia wasn't quite the stereotype South American villain. In fact the man looked prosperous. He was dressed stylishly in designer trousers and a blazer with a strange badge that looked like an insect.

Mrs Wenman smiled. 'I'll leave you to talk in private. Please ring if you would like a cup of tea.'

Marchway took the proffered hand. 'Mr Garcia, I'm sorry to disturb you today but you may be able to help me with some enquiries.'

'I am very happy to help you, Inspector.'

Marchway was surprised. This man spoke perfect English almost without accent.

'Yes,' Garcia continued. 'I think you want to hear what I know about the young lady Michelle Le Bois. You understand the woman was a nuisance but we never wished her dead.'

'Thank you, sir. What can you tell me?'

'I think you should know that unfortunately I suffered a financial loss last year. I became persona non gratia in my own homeland and Mrs Wenman offered me sanctuary.

'I am of course grateful to her and her father and I felt a little deceitful. You see I am taking steps to repair my fortunes. I own a tract of land in Chile and I have a licence to drill for oil. I was contacted by Mr Hengist Crickerman. You see I knew him as I am or was involved with yacht racing. Hengsit agreed to invest a large sum in my oil exploration provided I helped him in this foolish scheme of his to win a yacht race. Please understand I didn't approve of this conspiracy.'

Marchway could have made several comments at this point. His own researchers had told him that this man had been involved in an attempt to sabotage two Olympic medal winners. 'Where does Michelle Le Bois come into this?'

'She was Crickerman's agent. She was supposed to deal directly with Ollavasen the man who was bribed. But I can tell you Inspector the woman was a damned nuisance and one day she caused a very unpleasant scene.'

'Can you tell me some more about that?'

'Yes of course, but we never really understood what it was about. But one day a man rang at the gates and wanted to talk to Miss Le Bois. Mrs Wenman didn't see why not so the man was invited to walk up the drive. Michelle Le Bois became very angry and said we should never have let this man in. Then she said she'd talk to him but only on the lawn at the front. We watched from the window and Michelle began to rant and scream at this guy. We couldn't hear a word that was said but it was certainly very acrimonious. Then Michelle turned her back and stormed into the house. Mrs Wenman tried to find out what it was all about but Michelle became sullen and wouldn't speak. We assumed the man was an ex-lover but the boy working in the garden says not.'

'Why, and is he trustworthy?'

'I don't know him, but all he did was report words he heard.'

'Which were?'

'The boy claimed that Michelle called the visitor a murderer.'

'Please Mr Garcia, can you give me a name for this visitor?'

'No I'm sorry. I thought you might ask that but he never told us at the time and nor did Michelle. But the gardener did hear him say; "why do you keep threatening Nicky?"

Then Michelle shouted. "Because she's always defending that deceitful bitch".

'Then the gardener says the man yelled a lot of foul language and said. "I never did it, it wasn't me. Keep away from her – both of the girls" and a whole lot more that he didn't hear properly, but then the gardener says the man shouted. "Keep away or you may get it too.'

'Mr Garcia I know you only saw this intruder at a distance but can you give me a description?'

Garcia shook his head. 'He was probably of an age with Michelle: tall and very well built. We couldn't see much of him and he wore a cape with a hood. I think it is what you call colloquially a hoodie.'

'Can you recall the day or rather the date of this visit?'

'We may have a record somewhere of the exact date. It wasn't long after Michelle arrived here and she was still very nervous about something.'

'There's one thing I don't understand, Mr Garcia, sir. Why was Michelle Le Bois offered hospitality here?'

'She was to be the go-between to Ollavasen. I am afraid I was responsible for a bit of deception. I told Mrs Wenman that Michelle was an English niece and that she was involved in a business deal for me.'

Yes, Senor, thought Marchway. Deception is your forte.

'Dave, why are you so moody tonight?' Josie glared across the table. They were having their weekly meal out in their favourite restaurant. It was a relaxed evening that she looked forward to and now her partner seemed preoccupied and sullen.

'Sorry, my darling but I've got things on my mind.'

She smiled. 'In England we say, a trouble shared is a trouble halved.'

'It's this business with Crickerman. It's beginning to get to me.'

'Hey, you were over the moon yesterday. The Banner are giving you a pay rise. They're not trying to back out of it are they?'

'They'll deliver but only if I pursue this to the death and I'm not sure we've seen the last death either. God, Josie, I'd much rather be reporting the cricket test but they've delegated that to Brian.'

Josie was worried now. 'Dave, what do you mean more death?'

'What I mean is that out there somewhere is a mad person. Slipped their trolley is another thing you say in England. I've given that Inspector Welsh everything I've discovered. I've broken my promise to the Evans' and mentioned Senessen, but these police are that stupid. All I get is a pat on the head and a load of cop speak. You know the stuff, "we thank, you sir and we are pursuing all avenues". Look I'm a writer, even if I am a dumb Kiwi I write in English. Tell me, how in hell's name do you pursue an avenue?'

'But Dave, please, what do you mean by more death?'

'My intuition tells me that Crickerman is going to be the next. I don't like what I've heard about the man, but I don't want to wake up tomorrow and read that he's been knifed to death.'

# CHAPTER 25

Hengist Crickerman had lost blood but he was alive. He was bleeding from his neck and he could feel the blood leeching into the shirt around his right shoulder. At the London flat the police had been watching but not here. He had only wanted to be alone and he had paid for it.

With a struggle he managed to stand. The room spun around him and he felt sick but there twenty feet away was the telephone. Could he get there? Of course he fucking could. He was Hengist Crickerman and no homicidal little creeper was going to beat him. Nobody ever beat him least of all a mad nutter. He pressed the handkerchief tightly into the neck wound and slowly shuffled giddily to the phone table. He picked up the receiver and logged 999.

He stood long enough to hear that both police and ambulance were on their way and only then did he stagger and crash to the floor. As he lay there he remembered the crazy nutter's last screamed words. The screams were incoherent and what did they mean? Yes, the incident had been an embarrassment but he had compensated hadn't he? Forty thousand pounds and should have been the end of it. The world was going mad all around him and he'd done nothing wrong – nothing to deserve all this.


The Kent police and the casualty ambulance raced up the long drive within minutes of each other. The front door was locked but lights shone throughout the house.

'I'll go round this side,' shouted the constable to his companion. 'You go the other way.'

A minute later the first man called. 'There's a side door and it's open wide.'

The two policemen ran into the house closely followed by two paramedics. The body by the telephone was fully visible in the lighted room.

The paramedics ran and knelt down beside it. 'He's lost blood and he's unconscious but I think we'll save him.'

'We'll fetch a stretcher,' said the other paramedic,' and we'll put him on a drip. Is that Ok with you guys?'

'No, you go ahead,' said the first constable. 'This is going to be a crime scene but we don't want the man dead. Do your realise who that is?'

'No, but this is a classy house.'

'He's Crickerman the supermarket boss. I dunno' but they say he's one of the richest men in the world.'

'It seems we got this one wrong.' Inspector Welsh's chief was not friendly. 'I suppose you know the Australians regard this man as some sort of icon?'

'Yes, sir. But the evidence…'

'No, you had no evidence that would stand up in court. Why did you ignore the information from that journalist, Manning?'

'Please, sir,' Inspector Welsh seemed near to tears. 'Oh, please sir, Manning writes about boats and Rugby. How could he really know anything?'

'He gave you the same name that Crickerman has given us now he's conscious again. The suspect has since vanished.'

'But sir, Crickerman could still have killed Miss Logan. Your suspect had no quarrel with her.'

'No, Inspector, this is all speculation and we don't need speculation. From now this investigation is the priority of the Kent and Hampshire forces. So in the meantime what are you doing about the arson in Witherton Street?'

'I'll investigate it immediately, sir. You can rely on me.'

'Well go out and prove it.'

'Josie, this is bloody awful. I've got a really bad feeling about this.' Dave Manning turned to his partner. Josie had never seen him so agitated.

'Darling,' she stroked his head. 'There's nothing you can do.'

'Yes there is. I've just rung the police and given them the name. I am worried as to where that crazy psychopath is and what's going to happen next. I doubt the killing'll stop now.'

'He failed in Crickerman's case, though. Surely he'll run a mile and hide.'

'Josie, this isn't a rational being we're talking about, and I know the killer is obviously a warped psychopath.'

'But who, Dave and where would the killer go?'

'I've got an idea and I hope to God I'm wrong. Come on we're driving down to Hampshire.'

'I've cooked this,' said Kirsten. 'Steak and kidney pudding: it's Emily's favourite from when she was a kid. The poor girl's been run off her feet with baby care. We'll take this with us and she won't have to cook.'

'Tom's been doing some of the cooking, she told us,' Steve replied.

'Well this will give them both a break.'

The rain overnight had passed and the countryside was wet and smelt good. Kirsten drove through the neighbouring town of Petersfield and then out onto the A272 road for Alresford.

'I really feel for those two,' said Steve. 'You know, starting a family and then all this trouble on their doorstep.'

'Yes,' said Kirsten. 'It is such a co-incidence that two of the killings were people who wanted to hurt Emily.'

'I suppose the police have a job to do but in both cases they virtually accused Emily and Tom of having a hand in it. Luckily when the Le Bois woman was killed they were with us and when Smidgin was done to death they were in a public restaurant.'

'I know,' replied Kirsten. 'What is it about our family that all this trouble follows us everywhere we go?'

'I don't know and I wouldn't want to speculate about fate. But think of it, both Emily and Tom snatched as children by vile people.'

'Maybe it's the same fate that brought us together,' said Kirsten. 'Let's hope it'll leave us alone now.'

Just past the little village of Tichborne they slowed for a herd of cows. The lanes here were narrow but they were in no hurry. 'Tom's gone to work,' said Steve. 'But he said he'll be back by six.'

'Emily sounded excited on the phone. She says Peter spoke something. She wasn't sure quite what but if sounded like "glue".'

Steve laughed. 'That's a bad start. Maybe he'll be a bit messy and sticky.' For the first since the *Avocet* disaster he felt relaxed and happy. The sail making business had not suffered, for the first time in six years they had a full order book in four of the six Easterbroke branches. Emily was settled in her legal career and she had given them their first grandson. Her brother Johnny had just been accepted for university at Oxford. That was a big first for the family. They had certainly come a long-long way from his deprived childhood. He could scarcely believe it himself. Sporting honours, a successful international business and a knighthood. He wondered what his late parents would have said about that one.

It read five fifteen on the dashboard clock when they turned into the little unmade lane that led to Emily and Tom's cottage. Kirsten eased the car into the parking layby at the front gate and slid out of her seat to stand by the car. Steve took somewhat longer to leave the car. He still had many after effects of the stroke that had laid him low while sailing in Germany.

Kirsten had paused at the garden gate staring. 'What is that awful racket? That's never the baby.'

Steve could hear it now, a high pitched wailing; a mixture of pain and terror. 'Come on, someone's in big trouble.'

Kirsten ran up the path while Steve limped behind. Then he saw it in the garden. A figure was crouched clutching a bleeding arm while she howled and sobbed. She was Lily Lorrimer the couple's nanny.

Lily saw them and her screams turned to loud sobs while she shook convulsively. 'She's taken him. A woman – she's taken Peter and she's got a knife. She cut me because I wouldn't let him go.'

Steve was stunned he could hardly move or speak. As usual it was Kirsten who absorbed the crisis and took control. 'Lily where is Emily?'

'Oh, she chased after the woman and there's a knife.'

Kirsten knelt down beside the distraught Lily. 'Listen to me, how long ago was this?'

'I dunno', it was just now only minutes ago.'

'Which way did they go?'

'Up the track towards the farm.' Lily collapsed. 'Oh save him,' she sobbed. 'He's a little darling is Peter and he's never done anyone harm and everyone loves him.'

Inspector Marchway had his full team assembled and by God he had their attention this time. 'As you all know Mr Hengist Crickerman was attacked and badly wounded last night. The attacker entered his house while he happened to be alone and made a violent assault with a sharp knife. This assault has all the hallmarks of the previous murders to which this man was linked. It seems we have mentally-deranged criminal who has so far avoided us.' The room was still. They were all intent on his words.

He continued. 'From now on we are combining with the Kent force on a single investigation. We are dealing with what the media like to call a serial killer and that killer must be stopped. You have all been briefed on your separate roles. So Gentlemen, ladies go to it and good luck.'

The investigation team filed out of the room and Marchway turned to Superintendent Hollins who had been sitting beside him.

'Is there any progress on the Smidgin murder?' Hollins asked.

'No, sir, but I still have a feeling that we may find it to be the work of the same killer.'

'That's a big assumption, Garry. There isn't a shred of evidence to back it.'

'I know that, sir. Intuition – we're not supposed to use that, but I do make connections. Yachts have been bedevilling these investigations all along. Then Smidgin's openly threatens to hurt Mrs Stoneman. I still expect Smidgin's killer to have been someone in that room and someone determined to protect Mrs Stoneman.'

'If you're wrong about all being by one hand, then we've two mad persons on the rampage.'

'Well, sir. Let's hope that this time I'm right.'

Marchway's mobile phone was ringing. 'Yes,' he listened intently. 'Mr Manning, you may be right but we cannot act on the say so of a journalist. I agree, if you feel so strongly you must go to the house in question. If anything suspicious occurs you may report to me direct.' He slammed the phone into his pocket and swore. 'That bloody boat reporter, Manning thinks he's solved our murders and I have a nasty feeling he's beaten us to it.'


Dave and Josie had reached the cottage. 'That's Steve Simpson's Volvo, but why has he left both doors open?' He parked the car and jumped out. Josie followed and stood beside him. 'I don't like the look of this. I've got a bad feeling that we're too late. I wish I'd phoned Emily and told her who we think is the mad person.'

'The front door's wide open,' said Josie. 'Let's go give them a call.' She led the way up the path and into the house. 'Hi, anyone there?'

There came a moan from the kitchen. Both ran in there to see figure limp in a chair clutching a blood stained pad to her arm.

'Lily, what's wrong?' Josie knelt down beside Lily. 'Oh, what's happened?'

'She stabbed me, and she's stolen little Peter.'

'Who is this person, Lily?'

'It's that girl called Susie. I never liked her.'

'Where's Emily?'

'She's gone after them and so have Emily's mum and dad.'

'You should be in hospital,' said Josie. 'I'll ring for an ambulance.'

'Do that now,' said Dave. 'I'm going to find Emily.'

Josie felt fear now. 'Darling, be careful, that girl's mad and she's got a knife.'

'Maybe she has, but she's got Emily's baby and I'm going to stop her.'

Josie pulled out her mobile and dialled 999. 'Dave, what's the post code for this place?'

'In their office,' he called. 'There'll be letters on Tom's desk.' He left the room and vanished from the house.

Josie connected to the emergency services and told them the gist of what had happened and the location. She put down the phone and stumbled through the front door. Standing there was Tom with a look of bafflement on his face.

Emily was facing the second traumatic test of her short life. Suddenly all this made crazy sense. Why had no one realised who it was doing these killings? She was going to save her baby. She would save him. If she lost her life in so doing, she would save little Peter. Susanna was hampered by the weight of the child she carried in her arms and Emily began to close the gap.

'Susie,' she called. 'Stop we can talk.'

Susanna paused momentarily and then swerved into the little copse of ash trees beside the lane; Emily followed. Later she tried to analyse her feelings at that point. Somehow it was surreal, she seemed in a dream, but she knew what she had to do.

She was alone woman to woman. No men and no police. Either would spell disaster. She had to do this by her own wits and her own female guile and understanding. She was facing an unbalanced mass murderer; she could see that now. She remembered the rumours. Before the Atlantic race Ollavasen had tried to rape a girl. It had to be Susanna. Was it this that tipped her over the edge? Some said she was infatuated with Crickerman and yet she had tried to kill him. Susanna was a lesbian, she was Chloe's girl. Yet she seemed to have an appetite for men. Was it that the mental divide and torment that sparked the madness? All this stormed through Emily's mind. She must be detached as in a courtroom; be rational with the irrational.

'Emily that's far enough – you keep back,' Susanna had her knife and was holding it against Peter's throat. He showed no reaction and his little face looked almost contented.

'Susie, you mustn't hurt him – he's done nothing to you.'

'No, Emily, he's a baby. I had a baby and that man killed her. Why should you be happy when I'm not allowed to be?' Susanna was crying and her voice had a wild timbre, and now Peter was awake and also crying. Emily felt a mental stab wound. She must not move. She must stay calm. A sudden movement and her child might die. Only calm and reason would save him.

'Susie, I'm sorry. I didn't know about your baby. When was this?'

'In Australia.'

'Can you tell me?'

'Hengist made me pregnant. The he forced an abortion. She was going to be a little girl. I had passed the legal limit for abortion. Hengist bribed a clinic. He doped me and they did it.' The woman was weeping huge gasping sobs as she told the story.

'Susanna, that's horrible, it's evil. But surely you and Chloe could adopt a baby.'

'Oh sod Chloe. She's been boring me. I've done with her.'

Emily was thinking ahead. 'Susie, did you do something to protect me?'

'What d'you know about that?' Susanna had raised the knife again.

Oh, God help me, thought Emily. Have I blown it? Will I have to fight her? If I have to I'll let her use her knife on me and not Peter.

'That man in the pub was horrible,' said Susanna. 'He was going to hurt you and I wasn't going to let him. That Michelle too she hated you.'

'Thank you, Susie. That was kind of you.' Crazy answer but what else could she say?

'Susanna,' a man's voice shouted; a high pitched voice that cracked with an edge of panic. 'Put the baby on the ground and walk towards me.' It was Tom and Emily was appalled. How stupid could that man be? History was repeating itself in front of his eyes. Tom who aged ten had been abducted by another mad woman and threatened with death.

'Go away Tom Stoneman, Emily doesn't need you. She's going with me. Peter is going to be our baby.'

'I'm calling the police,' Tom shouted. He held his phone.

Emily reacted in desperation. 'No, Tom, not yet. Leave this to me.'

'She's right, Tom,' it was another man's voice and one of quiet authority – her own father. 'This is for Emily. She understands.' He turned and walked back towards the lane. 'Come on, Tom old man. Let her settle it.' Tom followed him looking back over his shoulder as he went. Emily threw him a quick smile. At the edge of the trees were three more people: her mother and Dave and Josie.

'Susanna, if you put Peter on the ground we can talk,' Emily called.

'Oh, Emily,' Susanna sobbed. 'If only you had seen that I love you. I loved you the moment I saw you. You me and the baby, we could have been so happy.' She placed Peter on the ground and then sagged to her knees, head in hands weeping without restraint.

Very slowly Emily walked the few yards to the spot were Susanna was swaying and moaning. Emily looked down at her. Then moving with more care and gentleness than she had shown in her life she bent down, took Susanna's hand and with all the tenderness she could muster she removed the knife. 'Come on Susie, let's go indoors and I'll make us a pot of tea.'

'Your Tom is going to fetch the police.' Susanna's tears had gone now. She spoke steadily and quietly. 'I never liked Tom. He's a misogynist.'

'Well, yes he is sometimes, but he has some good points.' Emily picked up her child cuddled him and whispered in his ear. Then she put her other arm around the woman's shoulders and they walked very slowly back to the cottage.

# CHAPTER 26

Tom also had memories. With awful clarity the years had spun back until he was once more a ten-year-old held in the grip of another mad woman. His step-father, the older Peter, had saved him that day with violence and now Emily, his lovely Emily had saved his son by her own wits and by her natural goodness. He, a grown man was dabbing away the tears that flowed down his face. The others with him, his parents-in-law and Dave and Josie were all in different ways affected. Steve was strong and reassuring, Kirsten was shaking. Dave Manning was silent but his face had an odd green tinge through his tan. His girlfriend Josie was weeping unrestrained.

Steve, despite his lameness set the pace back to the cottage. Tom now understood that. They must let Emily with Peter and that woman follow slowly. It was true Emily now had custody of the knife but they must not risk this Susanna having another spasm of madness.

An ambulance was pulling up in the roadside layby. Josie left them and ran on ahead. A minute later Tom could see her talking to the paramedics as they unloaded a stretcher and went into the cottage. They all stood and watched as poor Lily was carried into the security of the ambulance. It drove away down the lane and then they heard the siren blare as the driver turned towards the roundabout and Winchester.

Slowly the sad little group behind them caught up. Emily smiled wanly at Tom and shook her head. 'Tom, take Peter, please, he needs cleaning.'

As in a dream Tom obeyed and watched as Emily took the shuffling figure of Susanna into the kitchen. 'Susie and me are going to talk,' she said. 'Talk alone.' She laid the knife on the hall table and gave Tom a stare of command. 'Take Peter to the bathroom and clean him.' She shut the kitchen door behind her.

'Now we ring the police,' said Steve.

It was almost half and hour before a lone police car drove up the lane. Two uniformed policemen strode up to the door. Tom let them in just as Emily emerged from the kitchen. Visible was the figure of Susanna slumped over the kitchen table.

'All right,' said the first policeman. 'What's been going on here?'

Emily's laugh was shrill and wild. 'I thought coppers only said that on the telly.'

'What will happen to her now?' Tom looked at Chief Inspector Marchway.  Five hours had passed since the trauma of that afternoon. The inspector had asked for an informal visit.
    'I think your wife may be able to answer that better than I can.'
    Tom looked at Emily.
    'She's told me everything, no equivocation or hiding. If she makes the same  statement to your investigators and pleads guilty then I would guess the verdict will be mental instability or diminished responsibility and the sentence will be in Broadmoor or Rampton, but it will be life.'
    'Are you able to repeat what she told you?' asked Marchway. 'By the way I understand that Crickerman has identified his attacker.'
    'Yes,' Emily continued. 'There's no way I can be involved in the legal side nor probably can Tony Travis. Ollavasen's murder had nothing to do with the bribery. A day before the Atlantic race started from Plymouth, Ollavasen sexually assaulted Susanna. He would have raped her if four of his own crew hadn't broken it up.'
    'I know that,' said Marchway. 'I've a witness from Ollavasen's boat and he told me about it but he didn't name the girl. If only he had we might have cut short her mad spree. But that's the one murder we can prove no doubt. She left a DNA sample under Ollavasen's finger nails. When it's tested we will almost certainly find it's hers.'
    'Yes,' said Emily. 'But you'll need a confession for the other killings. She admitted to me how she did all of them but she could retract that. I've no witnesses to what was said.'
    'Apart from that,' said Marchway. 'Every time there's a violent unexplained crime we have unconnected nutters coming in to confess. Her defence counsel would use that.'
    'I have one piece of information,' said Dave. 'Susanna was seen near Greatswood on the day Michelle Le Bois was stabbed to death.'
    'How was this and why weren't we told?'
    'It was the man Philip Evans who found the body. He told me his wife was worried because he, Evans that is, had seen a person at West Meon he recognised from the sailing and who was about to walk down the Greatswood track. I told him to go to the police. Yesterday I rang Mrs Evans and she said her husband thought the person on the track to be harmless. Then she gave her husband's description of this person and it sounded like Susanna. She went down the track first but a little later Evans saw someone he recognised from the sailing scene and it

was Jason Senessen. Evans said they both arrived in the same car so it seems it was Senessen who met her in Petersfield and then drove Susanna to West Meon. That's when the alarm bells really sounded. I knew from my Australian investigation that Senessen had threatened Crickerman.'

'I did try to pass on my ideas' but your people were a bit negative,' Dave sounded angry

'It wouldn't be enough to convict,' said Marchway, 'but it would have helped us. We will pull in this Jason character; he might have witnessed the assault and then done a runner. Why did he drive the woman there? If he doesn't cooperate he'll be an accessory.'

'That's not all,' said Dave glanced at his friends. 'Do any of you remember that evening in the Ship at Itchenor?'

'Yes I do,' said Tom and the others nodded.

'I picked up a copy of the Banner with a headline about a supermarket boss and a stabbing. The Metropolitan police were playing that case very close and the Banner only had a very sketchy idea about what had happened. But Susanna knew. She blurted out something about the woman being "a waste of space, or no loss". I thought at the time; how the hell did she know who the victim was?'

'I wonder,' said Marchway. 'Sometimes these psychos have a wish to be caught. In some sick way they're proud of what they've done and want the world to know it.'

'I know,' said Dave. 'That thought had crossed my mind. But I do feel guilty that I didn't report to you what we found in Melbourne. I'm sorry but I was being the journalist with the hot story although I didn't realise it was that hot.'

'What happened?'

'We met Crickerman's wife and she told us about the pregnancy and the forced abortion. She didn't know the girl's name but they did at the yacht club. It was Susanna.'

'Emily,' Tom asked. 'Did she say why she killed Michelle Le Bois and the PA girl?'

'Jealousy – what I would only describe as upside down jealousy. In spite of everything he'd done to her she thought of Crickerman as her property. She resented Dione Logan but at the same time she thought Dione was disloyal because she was being abusive in public about the boss and she'd stopped going to bed with him. The Dione killing happened while Susanna was supposed to be in Kent with her parents. Parents, oh God what must they be going through and how in hell are we going to break it to Chloe?'

Tom looked even more puzzled. 'Why kill Le Bois. What had she to do with anything?'

'Susanna went looking for Michelle because she knew she was living at Greatswood. She only went to spy out the land so to speak but then by pure chance she saw Michelle on the footpath. We know Michelle was the go between to Ollavasen but as far as Susanna was concerned Michelle had insulted Crickerman by refusing to have sex with him.'

'That is crazy,' Tom muttered. 'Absolutely bloody crazy. No. there must have been more to it than that.' Tom knew his own wife too well. She was concealing something.

Emily shook her head. 'Well, she's certainly going to give the psychiatrists a run for their money. What worries me is that she went after Michelle when she was staying here. She'd gone shopping for all of us and she took hours. She said she had to go miles to Qualistores in Petersfield because she had this spending voucher. I thought at the time it was odd. There's a much bigger Qualistores in Winchester and anyway Petersfield's only twenty minutes or so away. I did nearly ask her if she'd had car trouble.'

'Emily.' Josie had joined the questioning. 'What about Smidgin. Why should she kill him just on impulse?'

Tom could feel for Emily. Her expression had briefly flickered into one of pain and embarrassment. 'She heard Smidgin threatening to hurt me. The sharp pointed curtain rod was lying on the grass outside the pub. She picked it up and followed him.'

Josie also had an intense expression. 'Why was she protecting you? For what reason?'

Tom saw the pain in Emily's face. He stood up and put an arm around her.

'Sorry Josie. She told me why and I may have to say it in evidence but not now. Not after everything that's happened.'

'That seems fair to me,' said Marchway. 'If the accused fails to explain I may ask you again. But I think we can all guess some of it.'

They said goodbye to the Chief Inspector and he promised to report unofficially on Susannah's interrogation.

'I feel awful about all this,' said Emily. 'The truth was staring us in the face and we didn't realise.'

'No, don't feel bad about it. You're all rational folk facing an irrational person.'

'There's one thing that's occurred to me,' said Dave. 'The Banner crime desk told me that everywhere there's been a killing the CCTV had been disabled and at Hamble the floodlights as well. Susanna is an electrician. She worked for her father and Emily; remember how she fixed the fault in your kitchen?'

Marchway faced Dave with an expression of mock severity. 'You, Sherlock seem to have been two jumps ahead of us throughout this business.'

'I realise that now. I'm sorry.'

'No, you're a journalist – just don't make it a habit.' Marchway left the house and waved to his bored looking driver. A second car had arrived and three policemen were carrying a coil of crime scene tape towards the copse. A bit late in the day, thought Dave.

'I think I'll make another pot of tea.' Emily seemed unnaturally calm. 'I hope we're not going to make this a life pattern.'

'How so?' asked Dave.

'Did you know that both Tom and I were abducted by mad people when we were children?'

'We knew you were, but we've never liked to ask you about it.'

'I don't mind. I've bored for England about it for years and I collaborated on the book.'

'But Tom,' said Josie. 'What happened to you?'

'A woman, just like today's tried to throw me over a cliff and herself too. My Dad Peter saved me but he got a shot gun blast for his pains.'

'A bit more than that,' said Emily. 'It was all filmed from a helicopter and we're talking about Tom's step-father Captain Peter Wilson. While Tom ran for safety he stood and invited the woman to use the shotgun on him instead. The first shot took him in the legs but the second cartridge was a dud. For that rescue they gave him the George Cross; very rare for a civilian in peace time.'

'You did the same thing for us today,' said Tom.

'I won't get a medal but I saved our little Peter and that's all that matters.'

'I think you should get the credit,' said Dave.

'No publicity, please Dave. We'll tell Peter when he's old enough to understand, but I don't want reporters hanging round here. I didn't do anything that any mother wouldn't do and think about poor Lily; she could have died. I promised I'd ring the hospital again.'

'How is she?' asked Josie.

'When I rang she'd just been admitted to A and E, but they think nothing life threatening. I hope they'll let us visit tomorrow.'

'Lily's very fond of Peter and she's a good friend,' said Tom.

'You'll probably think I'm a hard bitch,' said Emily.

'Only sometimes,' said her mother. 'Why this admission now?'

'Because in spite of everything we've been through I am beginning to feel bloody hungry. I haven't eaten a thing since breakfast. If Tom and I cobble something together would all of you like to join us?'

'You needn't do any cobbling,' said Kirsten. 'If you look in the back of the Volvo you'll see a giant steak and kidney pudding – your favourite and there's enough for all.'

Emily hugged her mother. 'Mum that's fantastic. But I think I'll give Peter his bottle before we eat. He's deserved it.'

'Steak and kidney sounds just right,' said Tom. 'But I think I'll have a stiff whisky first. What about the rest of you?'

## *CHAPTER 27*

'Two thousand pounds, two grand, that's my bonus from the Banner,' Dave put the phone down and grinned with delight. 'That's our fares paid for NZ and a nice little advance for the wedding.'

'Oh, Dave, have I told you I love you?' Josie ran and hugged him.

He kissed her. 'You have mentioned it but then you're a romantic novelist.'

'When do we go?' she nuzzled against his chest.

'We said probably hold the ceremony in Auckland in January. I know my Mum and Dad are preparing something.'

'Emily and Tom want to come and poor Chloe. It might cheer her up.'

'Yes,' said Dave. 'I'll get you to compile the UK guest list and I expect my sister'll do the NZ one. And there's one other person who asked and she can afford to come and give us a good gift.'

'Dave, that is mercenary. Who is this you're talking about?'

'I mean Donna, Hengist Crickerman's ex. We met her in Melbourne, remember?'

'Of course I do. I liked her.'

'Yes,' said Dave. 'From what I've heard Crickerman's back in his office harassing his staff. They say he's got a big fat dressing round his neck and shoulder; claims he's abstaining from women.'

'That won't last.'

'One other piece of news,' said Dave. 'Erich Shilltinberg's flying in from Zurich next Thursday and he says he's something to offer me.'

'That sounds tempting.'

'We're going with Emily and her dad to Branham Lake and they're going to put the old guy in a boat for the disabled.'

'Hmm,' said Josie. 'I'd like to meet him. A loveable Billionaire; that must be a first.'

Emily was in her parents' house in Sussex. She came back into the sitting room and dropped into an armchair.

'Any news?' asked her father.

'That was Tony. The hearing's next Monday but it's going to be a guilty plea and diminished responsibility.'

'So you won't be called as a witness.'

'No, it will all be a formality. But the press have got hold of my name. I didn't want that, but I'll have to give them some sort of account. The second call was Nicky Coulden. The police have released her boyfriend without charge. It seems this Jason was properly conned by Susie. She rang him on her mobile and asked him to give her a lift. My guess is that she didn't want her pickup truck seen at West Meon.'

'Why?' asked her father.

'It all goes back to the time in Melbourne. He and Nicky were so sorry for Susie. But he really didn't know what she was up to. It looks now as if she was really looking for Michelle and it wasn't just a coincidence. Guessing how her minds works I would say she wanted suspicion on Jason so she could complete the rest of her killings. Smidgin was the only one she didn't plan.'

Kirsten walked across and began to massage Emily's shoulders and neck. 'Emily can you tell us? Please, why did that woman kill Michelle and Smidgin?'

'Oh all right, if you must know. I've already told Tom and I got angry.'

'Poor Tom – why?'

'Because the fool thought it was funny for a few seconds and then reality kicked in. But I think he'd already guessed.'

'You can tell us,' said her father. 'No way will we laugh.'

'All the time Chloe and Susanna were staying with us Susanna kept following me around offering to help with housework and cooking and the rest, and it's true she fixed the electric. I'm not the gay way inclined and I just couldn't see that she was going sweet on me; but of course I can see it now. I can't read the signs as I would if she was a bloke. But when I followed her into that wood, after she snatched Peter, she shouted it aloud. She told me how Crickerman had doped her so he could abort their baby. Then she pours out a lot of stuff about…Oh bloody hell. How do I say this?'

'She declared her love?' asked Kirsten.

'Yes, she said she loved me and had from the moment we met. That's why she killed Smidgin because he was threatening me. She was in the pub and heard him. And later she told me the real reason she killed Michelle was to protect me. She heard us talking about Lily Lorrimer seeing Michelle. Jason Senessen also found out that Michelle was at Greatswood. It seems he even went and met her there. The butler overheard him threaten her. Jason told Susanna and he took her there, pointed her down that footpath, but he had no idea Susie wanted to kill the woman.'

'But she did kill her,' said Steve.

She wanted...' Emily's voice had dropped to a husky whisper. 'Susie wanted to take the baby and me.'

Kirsten hugged her daughter. Once again Emily was the little fourteen-year-old rescued from that blazing cottage.

'Emily,' her father intervened. 'The world is full of strange people and full of good ones too. You've been unlucky but you've so much to treasure. Tom is a good man, one of the best I know. You've a son and a great future in your profession and one more thing...'

'You Tom and Peter have all our love and support forever,' said Kirsten.

## *EPILOGUE*


*THE DAILY BANNER*
*Broadmoor for life for mad knife girl Susie.*
*Minimum term twenty five years.*
*Judge praises Emily our Olympic girl.*


*DAILY MAIL*
*Tory MPs protest at lenient sentence for knife girl.*
*No one is safe.*
*Calls to bring back hanging.*


*SYDNEY MORNING HERALD*
*Judge says Brits ill treated our Aussie Hengist.*
*Knife girl put away for good.*


*THE FINANCIAL TIMES*
*Share issue for Anglo Chilean Oil Company.*
*Chairman Primo Garcia announces billion dollar oil strike.*


**THE END**

**Reviews of *The Nemesis File* (continued):**

**Olympic sailor and coach: Cathy Foster, 11th Dec 2004**

Rarely have I read such a racy book!  It's carries you along at pace, and holds you fast until the very end.  Just then, you think that maybe this is getting far-fetched, but the punch-line pulls you up short, and makes you re-assess the characters and their relationship to events. Suddenly the plot hangs together again in a very satisfactory way, just as good detective stories should.

Instead of long descriptions to 'paint a picture' of all the venues and situations, the writing is succinct and carefully crafted to give the maximum impression for the minimum words.  This gives the book its fast tempo, yet nothing is lost because the accurate detailing of locations and action bonds the reader into plot.  As a past Olympic sailor myself, I know the sailing venues described in both Chichester Harbour and Copenhagen well, and I can reassure any future reader that the author has definitely done his research.  In addition, he's right – you do build life-long bonds with other British athletes and other countries' sailors when you are part of the Olympic team representing your country. It is a pleasure and highly unusual to read a book which describes the joys of sailing and racing so well.  Yet it's not a book about sailing, full of technicalities of the sport.  Sailing provides the background framework for a story of murder and blackmail where the investigation chases over four countries and three generations of lives. A thoroughly enjoyable read.

*Cathy Foster went to the Olympics in 1984 (finished 7$^{th}$ and made history as the first woman helm since the 2$^{nd}$ World War) and competed in two other Olympic campaigns, the last being 2002/3. She's a freelance Coach who specialises in top level racing, including Olympic and Paralympic sailors*